OTHER BOOKS BY VICTOR BROOK

The Fields of Lost Battles   1993 *(in Russian)*

The Veranda for Showers   1999   *(in Russian)*

Victor Brook

Hotel
"Million Monkeys"
and other stories

**Translated from the Russian
by Alexander Boguslawski**

FLAMINGO BOOKS
Boca Raton, Florida

Flamingo Books,
17033 Newport Club Drive,
Boca Raton, FL 33496.
(877)989-2929 (toll free)

Library of Congress Card Number: 00-102093

ISBN: 0-9678981-0-2

Printed in the U.S.A.

This book is for Elena,
my precious wife

I am deeply grateful to Alexander Boguslawski, my good friend and a person of many talents, for his involvement in many aspects of preparing these six stories for publication. I also wish to give special thanks to Paul Licata and Kay Davidson-Bond for their constant support, advice, and generous help with the translation.

... My hotel, *Million Monkeys,* is one of the most popular hotels in the world. All the richest people of the earth want to stay in the hotel with such a name. They're opening their wallets even more willingly when they find out that the hotel is aboard a schooner. Finally, they go completely crazy and give me their last cent when they realize whither we are sailing. . . .

CONTENTS

Introduction...11

Hotel "Million Monkeys"..........................19

Ten Past Ten..51

A Ceiling with Lizards............................81

The White-eyed Saleswoman..................101

A Veranda for Showers............................143

Vodka and Broads....................................175

INTRODUCTION

Readers unfamiliar with Russian literature will find Brook's stories a literary revelation. They are rich, slightly dark, and intense. They are not *puerile entertainment*, a category of fiction that currently enjoys such a great popularity. On the contrary, Brook's stories reflect the best traditions of classical Russian literature and contribute to the ongoing examination of those problems that haunt all human beings—unrequited love, loneliness, incompatibility, failure, despair, search for fulfillment, self-imposed exile, sexuality, death and the mercilessness of time. However, Brook enriches this tradition by his innovative style—a combination of almost surreal dreams, fantasies and exotic landscapes reminding one of Alexander Grin, an unjustly forgotten author of evocative novellas.

Victor Brook was born in St. Petersburg (formerly Leningrad), Russia. After graduating from the College of Construction, he worked in Tiumen (Siberia). At the age of nineteen, he became a reporter in the Novorossiisk newspaper and began writing fiction. Two years later, Brook entered the Department of Journalism at the Moscow State University. From 1969 to 1971, he was on assignment in India, representing the Ministry of Foreign Trade.

In 1972, he graduated from the University and decided to settle in a remote village to write a book about India. While there, he worked as a teacher of English and history. A year later, he moved back to Moscow and took a job as an editor for the publishing house Molodaya Gvardiya.

Soon, unwilling to collaborate with the official propaganda apparatus, Brook quit his editor's job and, like many other young artists, supported himself by trying a variety of low-paying jobs, from forest ranger, railway worker, stoker, truck loader, and baker to director of a House of Culture. His attempts to publish his stories were unsuccessful because of their non-conformist style and originality.

In 1979, Brook emigrated to the United States; he has lived in Los Angeles, Craftsbury (Vermont), Lake Placid, and, since 1995, in Boca Raton (Florida). In 1982, he published his first stories in the Paris-based Russian emigre journal *Echo* and, two years later, *Hotel "Million Monkeys"* appeared in the prestigious journal *Kontinent*.

In 1992, Brook returned to his homeland for a year. The visit led to the publication in Russia of a collection of stories and novellas under the title *The Fields of Lost Battles* (Trast-Imakom Publishers, Smolensk, 1993). Since then, many stories by Brook have appeared in Russian and emigre journals. In 1999, his second book, under the title *The Veranda for Showers*, was published in Moscow (Novosti Printing & Publishing House). This book includes several short stories and a novel, *Koza Roza*.

The years spent in India gave Brook abundant material to convert into brilliant literary vignettes. The carpet seller unfurling his wares in *The White-eyed Saleswoman*, the ominous street-theater play in *A Veranda for Showers*, the guest house in *A Ceiling with Lizards* or the monkeys on the roof and the journey to Goa in *Hotel "Million Monkeys,"* are few of the occasions when Brook astonishes the reader with images of crystalline clarity and pure poetic power.

The author's characters are complex; we often pity them, trying to understand their internal torments and sympathizing with their attempts either to escape the reality that surrounds them or to find solace in dreams and fantasies, or, when everything else fails, in alcohol.

The hero of *Hotel "Million Monkeys,"* a village teacher, searches for the beauty and poetry in life, for a paradise on earth, and tries to cope with his infatuation with one of his pupils. He finds escape in drunken revelries, imagining that he is a traveler in India or a companion of the daring, bold, determined and ultimately victorious Portuguese discoverer Vasco da Gama. Each time, when he is about to discover a secret of this other, beautiful and fulfilling life, he is interrupted by real life's pedestrian and prosaic events, by the trite and the shallow. He continues his search in drunken fantasies, but the glimpses of India he has allowed us to see, smell, and taste, are unforgettable. . . .

Alexandra, the heroine of *The White-eyed Saleswoman*, withdraws from her unhappy life to a remote village where she falls in love with another lonely and dejected soul—a teacher from Moscow who has come to her village. Both of them, the most intelligent, but, at the same time, the most vulnerable and fragile people in the village, Donat and Alexandra not only cannot understand each other, but they cannot communicate to each other what is most important in their lives. He becomes a village gigolo and she a dictatorial saleswoman.

A similar type of misunderstanding awaits the hero and the heroine of *A Ceiling with Lizards*. Even though they desperately try to find true love, they break down and give up at the moment when this love seems to be in sight, within their reach. They misinterpret each other's actions and raise between them a wall that neither can scale.

Although the adolescent hero of *Ten Past Ten* feels and behaves like other adolescents, many fragments of the story seem to indicate that he, too, will have difficulties communicating with women and finding perfect love. Through his disturbing and cruel fantasies, he discovers his sexuality and *grows up* during his illness.

Edward, in *A Veranda for Showers*, is killed in a hotel room because he is too self-absorbed to realize that by taking a picture of a beautiful Indian girl bathing on a veranda he has violated the ancient customs of another country. He does possess a special talent to notice those perfect moments when everything in the world *comes together*, but this astonishing ability does not make him happy or successful in life. At the time of his death, he is still searching for the meaning of his existence and true fulfillment.

The Russian hero of *Vodka and Broads*, Georgy Vampukha, is lazy, often drunk, and unable to fit into his adopted country, America, and yet, throughout his senseless and wasted life he stays relatively happy—probably happier than his hard-working, successful friend Tiurikov. Tiurikov cannot exist without visiting Vampukha from time to time and discussing, somewhat crudely, the two things a man needs to live happily— vodka and women.

This first translation of Brook's stories into English is not a literal word-for-word rendering of the original Russian texts, but rather an authorized English version. This version is a result of close collaboration between the translator and the author. The involvement of the author has to be especially acknowledged. Such an involvement leads to a much better translation because the translator can easily avoid many problems plaguing those translators who labor alone, unable to consult with the author, and who often misrepresent the author's ideas. A famous anecdote about the eager, but inexperienced translator from German who once rendered into English a work by some John Wolfwalker Goethe and entitled it *The Fist: One Tragedy*, comes immediately to mind.

Since fiction is a product of imagination and invention, and the language plays an integral part in formulating and expressing those imagined thoughts and ideas, the translator faces many risks trying to convey clearly and exactly the original intentions of the author. Having access to the author, especially when the author knows English and can appreciate the English version of his work, is reassuring. Such a collaboration frequently benefits the translator, the author, the work and, ultimately, the reader.

I hope that the result of my collaboration with Victor Brook will reveal to the reader the spiritual and philosophical depth of his stories. Therefore, I would like to express my deepest thanks to the author for his generous help. I am also greatly indebted to Leslie Poole and Professors Barbara Carson and Jill Jones for sharing their expertise in English language and for their ability to improve the consecutive drafts of the translation. I'd like to thank my wife, Kay, not only for being the first, most important, reader, but for letting me *steal* from her so much time we could have spent doing other things. And finally, my particular gratitude goes to my friend Professor Paul Licata who devoted countless hours to this project, editing the texts, discussing diction and idiomatic usage, literally living the life of the characters and, in the process, contributing invaluably to the best rendering of the rich language of Victor Brook. Needless to say, all the remaining errors are solely my responsibility.

Alexander Boguslawski
Professor of Russian studies
Rollins College
Winter Park, Florida

Hotel
"Million Monkeys"

Sailing the seas is necessary,
Living is not as necessary.

Ancient sailors' saying

1

Alone at last, the teacher took a few steps, frowning at the boards under his feet (as creaky and dirty as everything else in the village), looked through the window at the late fall, and turning abruptly, stared through his scratched eyeglass lenses at the empty classroom. Short and unattractive, in a dirty-brown jacket and poorly cleaned boots, he fit well into the scenery behind him: sagging log huts, sobbing sky, grimacing puddles, and crows flying off naked branches.

The teacher looked at one of the student desks and his eyes came to life. He approached the desk and got down on his knees. The old paint of the seat revealed everything that one would expect: a spider-web of cracks, ink spots, the name *Tolia* carved with a penknife, a scratch left by a nail, and a hole from a missing knot in the wood. Unwillingly, all these cracks, spots, and scratches began to fade, rubbed out by the image of a raspberry-red skirt.

The smell of the old paint transported the teacher into the semi-dark hall of his village house. He shuffled by the logs, passed the sacks with winter supplies, pulled the old door by its handle, and went blind from the unexpectedly bright September sun and everything it shone on. He cursed his shoddy bathrobe, his uncombed hair, unshaven face, and listless eyes dulled by reading. In front of him, just across the threshold, the sun was raining gold on a girl of about fifteen carrying a heavy mail bag. She was holding a letter for him. Squinting and feel-

ing too timid to look at her, the teacher glanced at his
dirty and threadbare slippers. Not far from them, beyond the wooden barrier of the threshold, two doll-like
shoes, scratched all over by the country life, huddled
together; out of them, reaching up from the ground towards the heavenly ideal of beauty, sprouted a pair of
legs with semi-womanly outlines, dressed in simple
ribbed hose. The knees were melting from shyness, trying to hide under the folds of a skirt colored like sweet
raspberries. A little bit to the side and higher, a semi-
transparent hand was hanging like a delicate toy; above
that began the typically Russian, boundless and bumpy
area of the father's gray padded jacket. Still higher, a
long and pale neck attempted to detach itself from the
collar, as a plant from the earth; the neck was topped by
a golden fog with unbearably huge eyes. He took the
letter; she smiled and wanted to say something, but did
not, only turned around too abruptly; her bag swung
widely; she bent forward to keep her balance, tripped,
froze for an instant, giggled, and turned in his direction
her golden, fresh, sweet face changed by the sun's re-
casting of shadows. . . .

The teacher heard resonant, deliberate, and oppres-
sive footsteps in the school corridor. Only a guard, a
stoker, or a headmaster would walk like that around
school. Recoiling from his memories, the teacher rose
and straightened up his clothes just in time, so that the
director's head, which appeared in the doorway, found
him strolling absentmindedly among the desks. The head
was small, covered by puny grass ruffled up by variable
winds, with a thick web of wrinkles and a pair of pink
little eyes haphazardly slapped on it. The eyes simultaneously looked at and beyond him. The teacher emerged

from this *at* and *beyond,* and the director moved entirely into the classroom. He was small, thin, and wrinkled, but he wore a suit made for a muscular man, and put on airs of an intellectual and a boss.

"So where are the pupils?" the director asked sternly. "You let them go? You shouldn't have. That's bad. They'll get in trouble. They'll get drunk and the bigwigs will blame us."

"They already got drunk," said the teacher. "Right here in the classroom. That's why I let them go."

"Did you take away the bottle? Who had it?"

"I heard gurgling in every corner," the teacher answered apathetically.

The director jumped up, sat on the table, lit a cigarette, and squinted his eyes at the boring courtyard on the other side of the window.

"So you say you couldn't tell who the culprit was? Too bad you did not find out. There could be serious consequences. Let me give you an example. A bunch of 6th-graders polish off a bottle in class. During recess they find an axe. They shove one girl onto a desk. Bend her head, like a chicken's. And they axe off her braid, just like that. I ask them later, why? Just for the heck of it, they say. Or take the recent Moldavians. Electricians. They were putting up an electric line in the woods and ran into the kids. They organized a picnic—drank wine and fooled around. Guess, with whom? With your 8th grade girls."

The teacher shuddered; his face became ashen.

"With whom specifically?"

"All of them were there."

"And . . . your daughter too?"

"Katukha too." The director covered himself up with white smoke.

"And . . . Natasha?"

"All of them," said the director.

2

First, the axe killed the pine tree, then it chopped off its arms and its head, then carelessly peeled off its skin, examined the long, naked bone and jumped away to another tree. Sometime later, collective farm workers in gray, dirty padded jackets picked up the darkened bones. Incessantly paddling with their unshaven jaws in a stream of obscenities, the workers piled the bones onto a cart and drove them for a long time over moss and protruding roots, over the treacherous river bed, and along the main street flooded with mud. The iron beast, covered in axle-grease and mud and perhaps washed only by the rains and the workers' urine, performed heroic miracles. Its cabin was ready to cave in from the swearing of those who were riding on top of the bones. Tossed, banged up and chilled, the workers imagined that they were riding a tank through Germany and that the foreign vistas around them were reflected in puddles of Nazi blood. Finally, the tractor turned sharply into a vacant lot. All the workers gasped and jumped up in horror, but their faces lit up when they realized that the bluish bottles of vodka held by someone who had just narrowly escaped the tractor's chains were not broken, but merely splashed with mud. The workers quickly dropped the bones on the spot of future life cycles and even more quickly took care of the vodka. Then, for about three months, they did not hurry anywhere at all.

They would fly up to the bones every morning and, accompanied by the cozy smoke from the stove, they would gather in a friendly flock, swearing about this and that while the owner of the bones kept bringing them vodka, his wife kept cooking, and his kids kept helping out. And every time when the day went to sleep and the night woke up, tipsy, full, and satisfied workers would fly away, one by one, in various directions. Someday, in their old age, looking back at their lives, they would shed a tear over those wonderful times, wonderful even during rains and blizzards, and they'd perhaps decide that what happened in those days was the very happiness each of them was looking for, but at the time they didn't understand it because then they were just feeling good.

The workers intended to waste away at least one more month living such a happy-go-lucky, drunken, and satiated life, when suddenly, one dank morning, when all living creatures drag their legs along only to heal their hangover, the owner of the bones, instead of full glasses, extended towards the workers his ominously obscene fist. He could have simply made the gesture and a bit later he could have handed them the glasses as was customary; then everyone would have laughed it off as nothing, but a joke. Yet, for some reason, the fist did not disappear, but continued to aim at them threateningly.

"Fine, go to hell, you motherfucker," said the workers gloomily.

Furious, the owner bared his teeth and wheezed out, "You promised; three months have gone by, and you've only eaten, drunk, and talked; the rains are coming soon, so get going." (To protect the reader from additional indecencies, his words have been edited beyond recognition, only the meaning has been preserved).

The workers protested with hangover vehemence and, restraining themselves from beating him up, went slouching away. The owner of the bones knew the Russian soul; he stood there patiently and waited for one of them to turn around. And when his waiting paid off, he pulled a bottle out of the warm cellar of his bosom and waved the vodka about as if it were a flag.

By nightfall the frame of the house was almost ready. The workers generously washed it with vodka, piss, and vomit. The owner of the frame almost fell into the shavings, but the workers caught him just in time and asked him to pay up. They found the money in his foot bindings and kept counting it until the first cock crowed, until the bodies, rubles, and shavings got all mixed up, and until everybody decided morning is wiser than evening. In the morning, they beat up the owner for coming up short and for his unwillingness to make the hangover remedy available right away. But these were just details, trifles. The main thing was that the frame, on the brink of becoming a house, stood in the middle of Russia and through the empty sockets of its windows saw Russia's strange future, the fate of its future dwellers, and a teacher of Russian language lying in dirty boots on a squeaking iron cot supplied by the village Soviet.

That's how this house appeared here and what these logs have absorbed, the teacher thought, looking at the ceiling. He had been lying like that since he came back from school after learning the visiting Moldavians had defiled his love. This is the cause of my anguish. I felt anguish in the capital too, that's true, but of a different sort. It wasn't as numbing as here because sometimes an unexpected wonderful conversation, a rare book or a childhood friend interrupted it. But I was definitely unhappy in the city. The city did not have enough depth, purity, or that sort of dreamy peace, which, like lazy waves, spills over the pages of many classical Russian novels. I left hoping to find them in the country and instead found myself surrounded by decay, by wandering drunken peasants with no ambitions or hopes, by exhausted women and by little devils begotten in vodka, obscenities and faithlessness. Where are you, Russia? Are you alive? Because if this is indeed Russia, then I do not need it. Here, I will become a drunk or I will be killed by one. Like some unidentifiable insect. I would have left this village two weeks after my arrival, but the mailwoman got sick and Natasha, her daughter, delivered the letter. The girl instantly became my dream, my hope, *my spirit of Russian beauty*, as Pushkin would have said, and she has kept me here for the last three months.

He turned over and bit his pillow. Oh, my little mail girl! Why did you hold me back? Just to bring me another disheartening letter, which would declare that purity, sanctity, or hope no longer existed in this world? What did the Moldavian do to seduce you? Perhaps electricity helped him? His fingers touched you, like raw wires; his lips were hard as clamps; his haystack of hair sparkled and cracked and blue flames flickered in his eyes. Be damned, you electrician; be damned, all electricity.

It's time to get up and drink some water. My mouth is all dry and bitter. Yes, tomorrow is a holiday, the anniversary of the Great Revolution. There will be drinking in all the houses. I'll drink too.

Half an hour later, he was sitting in a corner between the table, stove, and window. He was looking at the dark clouds, at the rusty branches, almost transparent because

of their decimated leaves, at the thin, low fence, at the
boarded up windows of the sturdy-looking house next
door, at the scraggly black bird, as immobile as a scare-
crow, that recently appeared on the roof, and at the pole
resembling the letter *A* with four wires. Then his eyes
moved inside, to the dried-up flies on the window sill,
to the unintelligible pattern of the wallpaper, to the bowls
with salted cabbage, cold potatoes, lard, and bread, to
the bottle of *Moskovskaya* and to the empty, faceted glass.

He just wanted to sit in the darkness of the quiet hut,
surrounded by dark logs that were once pine trees, pen-
sive gloomy beings; he just wanted to sit and let his eyes
wander, to see simple, understandable things, to feel how
the blood carries the vodka through his body, dissolving
everything, relaxing it and putting it back in place, and
to hear—unexpectedly—a delicate, almost inaudible
ringing of a million syncopated drops in a quiet river.
He'd huddle up, strain, slow down his breath, listen carefully to the ringing, make an effort, submerge in it, and
get carried away by the lazy current, ringing quietly and
gently. . . .

3

I will sit under the ancient tree in solitude and darkness with a bottle of fragrant rum. Like a curious, invisible beast, I'll look at the lights of the hotel, at the candles
in front of the blurred faces, and at the quick-moving
silhouettes of the servants. I will hear muffled voices,
women's laughter, a hundred thousand cicadas, bursts
of some heart-rending Eastern melody and the sleepy
cries of a monkey or a bird.

A waiter will approach my table for the countless time to find out if I am finally hungry enough to order.

"No, not enough," I'll say. "I am still in my favorite state. It descended on me as a colorful, magical cloud, and it froze suddenly, so that I was constrained by a sweet, delicate daze. I am even afraid to sigh any deeper, to turn around, and to look at the menu; even talking to you I'm just barely moving my lips. So, please go away."

He will go away and his silhouette will burn down in the bright lights of the hotel. Once again, I'll be left alone with the ancient and wise tree. From my unearthly daydream, I'll listen to the quiet rustling of the tree's crown, breathe in the fragrance of its flowers and look at the ashen reflection of the moon, pensively swinging on the leaves. My heart will begin to beat harder. Yes, this is the sign; I've been waiting for it a long time; this is the moment to ask eternity the Main Question.

"Tell me, Honorable Tree, *how can I find paradise on earth?*"

The leaves will rustle in a special way, the moon will draw signs on the leaves, and the flowers will smell of something strangely familiar. Greedily and carefully, I'll heed them. . . .

"I know that you prefer solitude, but since today the hotel is overbooked, can I sit a few other people here?"

The cloud will crunch and dissolve; the daydream will crack and fall off, like a sweet, tight shell. I will look at the waiter morosely, and shrug my shoulders. The scoundrel will nod, run to the hotel, and have no idea that with his trivial concerns he has interfered in my attempt to guess the answer of the ancient tree. Now, a group of hungry engineers or a family with kids and aunts will come; they will chatter, suck their fingers, chew loudly, hiccup, burp, fret, and endlessly stare at me.

The waiter will bring a table and chairs. Soon, four silhouettes will approach. The rustle of dresses. The squeaking of chairs. The scratch of a match. The first match will break. The next one will emit sparkling smoke. The third will light the candle, illuminating the face of a young woman and two blonde girls in hats.

I will fall in love with this woman at first sight. We'll sit in the circle of the same tree crown and just one candle will burn for us; we'll have to get acquainted. I'll realize with horror that I am walking to her table.

"Excuse me," I'll wheeze or croak out, "Would you like to try some rum?"

Instead of splashing Coca-Cola in my face, she'll smile cheerfully and ask me to bring my chair over. I'll bring it immediately and sit down. It will become my sturdy raft. I'll push myself away from the shore and, steering confidently, I'll speed down the rapidly rushing river God only knows where.

"When the candle was lit in front of you," I'll begin, with confidence and inspiration, "it seemed to me that I was looking at a scene from an old English novel. You are English, aren't you?"

She will nod, rest her chin on her hand and get ready to listen again. Her beautiful face, illuminated from below. . . . The ropes of my raft will turn out to be rotten, and it will fall apart; I'll lose my balance, gasp for air, and drink some more rum. She will be too beautiful for me, and an overabundance of female beauty requires an overabundance of male self-confidence, which, excuse me, I do not possess. She will see me, a miserable being, convulsively holding on to a log carried away by the

fast-flowing river, and from the safety of the shore she
will throw me a rope in the form of a question:

"And, judging by your accent, you're probably a
Swede?"

"I am Russian."

"Ah yes, a tourist?"

"No, not a tourist. I am. . . ."

Oh God, how can I learn to answer straightforwardly
and confidently that I'm constantly searching all over
for paradise on earth. And that all the other labels, like
tourist, teacher, and citizen, are as stupid as, let's say, a
late sleeper. How can I explain to you, stranger, that
you've appeared to me because at this moment in my
life I'm disappointed by my search for paradise in the
present and I'm trying to find it in the future?

"I'm here on business," I will lie. "And how did you
happen to come to India?"

"We sailed on a ship." She'll laugh and throw her head
back. Her light hair will bounce furiously and a jewel
will sparkle in her earring. "We stop wherever we want
and for as long as we want. I'm enchanted by this country. Even by its smell and poverty."

She will cover her daughter's hand with her own,
"Girls, please tell the Russian gentleman, do you like
India?"

"Oh, yes, very much," the girls will whisper.

"It was Kipling who infected them with India. You
know," she'll turn towards me again, "I am crazy about
traveling."

The glass will squeak in my hands. The dark, yellow
candle flame will quiver and disintegrate. I'll watch carefully how the flame breaks apart. I'm forty five years old
and slightly bald; I already have a little pot belly and

failing eyesight; I've read half of all the books ever written; I've loved a lot, even if unrequitedly; I've thought
about everything; I've suffered for everyone—yet I
haven't had a chance to travel around the world. I'll remove my hand from the glass. The splinters of the fire
will reconnect and the amber flame in my rum will calmly
burn again.

"I'm also crazy about traveling," I'll say in a muffled
voice, and, after a while, I'll ask, "What did you like most
in India?"

"Goa!" She'll exclaim with confidence. "You haven't
been there? A wonderful place! A former Portuguese
colony. Imagine the city of Pandjim: an azure bay among
green hills, deserted beaches with white sand, boats with
torn sails, a monument to Vasco da Gama on the shore,
enchanting taverns, a lot of cheap, fresh fish; whisky and
rum also cheap. . . ." She'll grow silent, looking through
me at the former Portuguese colony.

I've already mentioned that she'll turn out to be too
beautiful for my ugly and shy self. But I'll assure myself
that it doesn't matter what I'm like, that all this is happening in my imagination because where else, but in the
world of fantasies, can the ugly and shy recoup their
losses? "Don't worry what you're like," the rum will
whisper, "rely on me, do you understand?" The other,
brave I, and my buddy Rum will obtrusively squeeze
my shoulders, slap me on the back and, blowing hot
breath into my ears, they will praise me, encourage me,
swear at me and make various hints. But all in vain. Pres-
sured by them, I'll cast glances at her and every time I'll
unfailingly get burned and dive into my glass to cool
off. Once there, I'll thrash around—until instead of me
Goa will sit down in front of her. Only then I'll recoup

my losses. I'll throw myself into these absentminded eyes, catch her running across a field, tumble her into the flowers and do it all.

All of a sudden, she'll notice me again; I'll get burned, break away, and begin to thrash around in the glass. I'll look at her timidly; she'll squint and smile weakly, but devilishly; I'll sweat, cool down, and the glass will yelp under my tightly clenching fingers. She'll look at the bill, take out her money, get up and smile politely.

"Thanks for the rum and the company."

Standing up, I'll follow them with my eyes. Trees, lights, and various other shadows will eventually wash away their silhouettes.

"Thank you," I'll say to the ancient tree. "Tomorrow morning I'm going to Goa."

4

It seemed the sound appeared long ago, but the other sounds, the sounds from the future, were stronger. At a certain moment, the sound broke through the teacher's consciousness, and it turned out that somewhere far away someone was knocking resonantly and deliberately. The teacher poured some more vodka. It gurgled noisily. And again a measured knock. Too bad there is nothing for a chaser. The teacher drank up. What abomination! Greedily, he bit some bread. The objects around him kept flickering, dissolving, and sometimes circling quietly, but the sound resembled a distant knocking heart. Maybe I am the only one who hears it? Maybe it is knocking for me? Maybe I should get up right away, leave the house and start walking—straight across the rivers, forests, mountains, and oceans? Maybe therein lies the

meaning of my life? Concentrating, as if he were sum-
moning up spirits, he stared at the empty glass. Its edges
were shaking and dissolving. At last, they rang out and
melted away. . . .

5

Groping around, staggering, I'll walk to my bed,
throw off my clothes into the dark night and fall into the
stormy world of dream visions. There, I will immediately meet Vasco da Gama and we'll sail to discover the
passage to India. We'll step ashore near Goa and be struck
by the beauty of the surroundings. "Would you like some
rum?" I'll ask Vasco. He will not answer. I'll turn around.
He'll be standing on a pedestal. I'll hear an inexplicable
worrisome rumble. Forcing my way through the sticky
air, I'll run back to our boat. The rumble behind me will
become louder and I'll try to run faster. Finally, I'll see
the shore. But the boat will not be there. A huge wave
will rear up and fall down. Swimming won't save me.
I'll turn around. Cannibals with rotted, bloodied mouths
will be running towards me. A drum made of human
skin will be hanging from the neck of each cannibal, and
each savage will be pounding on his drum with a human bone.

Merciful, the sand will allow me to fall into the semi-
darkness of my hotel room. I will sit up and moan, all
wet, staring at the fuzzy fan stirring the dove-colored
whites of the dawn. I'll breathe with relief, guzzle half a
carafe of water, wrap myself up in the chewed-up sheet,
close my eyes and listen, without falling asleep, to the
rumble above my head, imagining all kinds of nonsense.
The same cannibals with drums will be dancing around

a fire and I, of course, will be roasting on the spit. Air-planes will be dropping gravel. The local homeless poor will be stealing the iron sheets from the rooftop. Mon-keys will be playing tag on the roof. . . . This, however, will be reality, not fantasy. Their troop lives up in the tree crowns above the hotel. At dawn, barely awake, they begin to play tag. They fly after each other on springy branches. Spreading their paws widely and tenaciously, they fly unbelievable distances between trees, no matter how far apart they are. They rush towards the clamor-ing iron roof only to bounce off it, like ping-pong balls, towards any branch, from the thickest to the thinnest, and to ascend that branch perhaps as far as the moon. Isn't it strange that if the same clamoring were to occur at some dacha in Saltykovka, the monkey tag game would have been sheer fantasy. Ah, it's a futile pursuit to try to separate reality from fantasy; it's an unneces-sary confusion of thoughts. Lie underneath the clamor and believe that the door of the airplane, loaded with gravel, opened slightly, and the tiny rocks are dropping onto the roof. . . .

"Ta-ta-ta-ta-ta," the monkey paws will drum. "Vas-co-da-Ga-ma," I'll hear. What do I know about Vasco da Gama?

An old geography textbook filled with the mire of names and dates will float up from my childhood. I, a student of such and such a grade, will bend over the flattened planet and my glance will be caught and lead along the lines drawn on blue oceans. One of these lines will begin in Portugal on July 8, 1497, submerge itself in the Atlantic ocean, descend raggedly along Africa, circle the Cape of Good Hope, cut across the Indian Ocean, and, on May 20, 1498, will bury itself in the western shore of India. With burning envy, I'll keep bending over the flight of the chopped-down masts, over the mutinies of the crews, over the daggers held in teeth, over the thirst, scurvy, fever and over the hook-nosed face shaken by the shout "Land!" Following this line of his life, Vasco da Gama lost his ship and 105 men of his crew. But with the same line he opened the sea passage to India, defined Africa's outlines and proved the Indian sea to be an ocean. The second time, he went to India with 13 warships, brought back rich tribute to his king, and was made a count. The third time, he came to India as its viceroy. Now, that's living, gentlemen!

Finally, the clamor will cease. The monkeys will sit down to breakfast. Apparently, the sporadic knocks on the roof will be produced by falling leftovers, but I will be able to sleep while they occur and I will sleep till I hear the knock on the door. The servant will bring my morning tea.

"I hope you'll be stopping here again soon. Yes?" the owner of the hotel will inquire, hoping for a nod from me and quickly calculating my bill.

"Of course, Mr. Verma. I like the hotel. The monkeys alone are worth a lot."

"Oh, in India there are many hotels with monkeys. In our country one only needs to whistle and a million monkeys come running."

"A million monkeys! I've got an idea. Call your hotel *Million Monkeys* and you'll make millions."

"Hah, hah. I'll think about that."

"Don't forget a spare million for the idea."

"Hah, hah, absolutely. What will you do with the million?"

"Most likely, I'll buy myself a sailboat. Maybe it'll finally help me find paradise on earth."

"Hah, hah. You owe 347 rupees and 85 pice."

Life is miserly when it comes to giving people the gift of feeling the fullness of life. Many never receive it. I think that travelers receive it most often and I'll receive it too, as soon as an exotic ancient land begins to move fast under my wheels. It will look as if huge approaching trucks were going to jump at me, but they'll give way at the last moment. Thoughtful oxen and buffalo, and bullock carts on wooden wheels will carry their masters slowly and solemnly down the hot and dusty road of life. Wise goats will calmly walk away to the nearest shoulder of the road while homeless white cows and emaciated dogs, as always, will frantically try to choose its safer side. Bronze-faced people in loose clothing will drink tea with milk in the tireless shade of trees. A temple, forgotten by time, will appear and disappear, also of no use to me. A flock of macaques chewing their bananas will glower at me, run away and, cursed by the foreigner's memory, will never be able to do anything else, but chew and glower. A small river will shimmer in the sun; in it, I'll see heads of buffalo and figures of young girls washing clothes. A group of griffons will discuss where to look for fresh carrion. I'll catch up with, pass, and feel pity for a 1,000-year-old elephant that has absurdly become a slave of the human-faced fly sitting on its back. A young woman in rags, elegant as a movie star, with a baby comfortably straddling her hip, will look over her shoulder at the foreign prince and the prince will speed away into a beautiful life, while she, aging quickly, will continue to carry a heavy sack of grain on her head. A green parrot will fly from one fairy tale into another, crossing the road between them.

In the shade of a banyan tree as big as a square, the pupils will sit on the ground, and while I have them in sight, their teacher will probably be explaining that Vasco da Gama was not such a great man after all. "With him, dear children, began the plundering and enslaving of the Indian people by the Portuguese and the English," she will point at me, "like that one". The children will turn to look at me; I'll blush, turn my eyes away and speed up to continue the politics of veiled colonialism.

Yes, that's right, dear Vasco, in life it is always like that—for the same thing some people love you and some don't. That teacher hates you while I adore you, even though I'm not a Portuguese or an Englishman; nor even a geographer or historian. I adore you not for your discoveries, not for your shipholds filled with emeralds, not for the title of viceroy, not for the strength of your character and not for your unquestioned bravery and courage. I adore you for the simple reason that with one swing of your sailor's boot you were able to kick aside, like an empty can, domestic bliss, peace, success, security, family happiness, and concerns about old age and health. You ran aboard a schooner and raced to meet storms, reefs and cannibals. And it does not matter that you've been commissioned to find the road to treasures, but that you've understood very well that in order to discover something new, one must fearlessly and decisively, with a spark in one's eyes, push off the old; one must become a free bird and fly, and only then might a treasure island appear in the rips between the rolling clouds.

At seventy miles per hour, I'll fly into the unknown; I'll enthusiastically look around this exotic space and I'll feel alive.

The ravines will begin to slice up the plain; hills will appear on the horizon; the number of trees will increase and the road will start weaving. This means that soon there will be the mountain range and beyond the mountains—Goa. In the most desolate place, the three bandits borne by the long road—exhaustion, thirst, and hunger—will try to ambush me. Without reducing my speed, I'll check the map. To reach Goa, I must still drive and drive, mostly up the mountain winding road. I'll imagine how there, in the clouds, on a sharp cliff, in cold thinned air, I'll get carsick and nauseous and throw up the remains of my breakfast. I wonder—I'll swallow nervously and with difficulty—what could be hiding in those two yellow dots, that is, in those two tiny settlements? Should I have a bite there? In the yellow dot that is nearer, I'll imagine a dirty tavern, and inside, a rag of a menu in a local language, as well as a thin, muddle-headed waiter with his two-word (*yes* and *sir*) storehouse of English. I'll point at random to three things in the menu, and after ordering also *tanda pani*, a glass of cold, muddy water, I'll wait for the three losing cards. I'll be unbelievably lucky if one of those three dishes turns out to be gray, salty-sour, and very peppery yoghurt. I will not dare to touch the other two: a small clay pot with bright yellow pods in tar, and a pot with a brownish-green substance.

The bandits will finally slash me all over with their knives, especially around my stomach and my throat, when suddenly the nearest yellow dot will jump out from around the curve of the road and a little town will envelop and deafen me. There it is, packed with dust, heat, cows, goats, dogs, naked babies, loiterers and little shops full of everything in the world, but nothing worth buying. After driving by a couple of taverns, in which one or two customers will know what to do with the little pots, I'll see a sign *The Lilac Bar*. I'll turn around squealing my tires and raising clouds of dust; I'll abandon the car next to a bull gloomily cooling off on the road. I'll read the sign once more and, not believing at all that this is a *bar*, and even more, a *lilac* bar, I'll open the entrance door.

6

Knocking. It's gotten dark. And, except for the knocking, it's quiet. How strange that this evening not even one sound of a drunken scream was heard outside, no scrap of table laughter leapt out from the slightly opened door, no woman guffawed and no children scurried by with halting voices and out of breath. What a mysterious silence on the eve of a national holiday. Maybe here they always celebrate holidays this way—they drink in silence until they pass out. Or perhaps. . . . Oh yes—I had forgotten about it because of the news about Natasha—there is a special meeting tonight. Abram Serafimovich, the party chairman, is standing on his healthy leg behind the lectern that is supported on both sides by his crutches. Reading a one-hour abstract about the revolution, he sternly scrutinizes the audience, looking over the top of his glasses, lifting his finger in the air and clinking with his war-time medals. It is decent and quiet in the club. One can only hear the polite squeaking of chairs and discreet coughing; in general, a Russian is well-behaved and patient when he is wearing his best suit, and when he anticipates a bottle of vodka and pickled mushrooms.

Knock . . . knock . . . knock . . . knock. . . . It sounds as if you were lying in the earth listening to an elderly, sober peasant trying to dig you up. The soil is firmly packed, dry. The peasant is pounding it with a pick-axe. If I were to go in the direction of the knocking, I could find out what it meant. Let's assume that someone is making an awning. Boring. I'd rather sit in the dark, drink vodka and let my imagination soar.

In the middle of the street stands a mountain of a bull. Its legs resemble four inclined posts. Its head hangs to the ground. Its horns sparkle menacingly. Between them is a bloody porridge. A hammer methodically falls in it and the porridge sputters in all directions. Blood runs in a narrow stream to the nostrils, washes them off and spills into a dusty puddle on the road. The hammer is covered with dried-up and fresh pieces of pulped skin and hair. The pants and the shirt of the peasant are all covered with blood. He throws the hammer aside and walks away. He stands there, steaming, drunk, staggering, watching how another peasant, exactly like him, grabs the hammer, walks over to the bull, lifts the hammer, and squats; the hammer flashes and sinks into the forehead. Crack! The bull sways ever so slightly and keeps standing as if it were implanted in the ground.

My friend who has just arrived from Moscow may also hear the knocking and ask me, "Say, what kind of noise is this?" "A common occurrence," I'll tell him nonchalantly. "The peasants are pounding a bull." "What?" My friend will get anxious. "Oh, it's nothing, don't pay any attention to it; let's have another drink."

The friend will jump out of the hut. He'll be back soon. "There is no bull out there, they're nailing together an awning. Why did you kid me?" "I did not kid you, reality did. I merely superimposed on its faded paint a couple of fresh brush strokes and an unusual picture came out; it made us both worry so much that you even abandoned the light and warmth and ran into the dirty darkness to admire, as you thought, the original. Therefore, I conclude that through my mouth God breathed beauty into the gray rock laying inconspicuously in the middle of the world, and the rock became beautiful and fragile, like all Universal beauty, but in that dirty darkness you found the peasant who was gloomily nailing together an awning for his chilled emaciated cow, and you jumped back in disgust, you squashed the beauty with your muddy boots, you mixed the beauty with the mud, and now you sit here disappointed and angry. I do not know why, but many people (I am afraid of the word *majority*), seem to have been born to insult beauty, that is, to destroy that, which constitutes the foundation of happiness. And what does this mean?" I will ask my friend. "It means," I'll answer impatiently, "that the Lord lovingly fertilized, tilled, and planted with the seeds of beauty and happiness a parcel of life for every man, but some powers, obviously evil, make people mercilessly pull out the Lord's beautiful plantings and diligently pamper the leftover weeds. And since I am afraid that I may be doing the same thing, I'm trying to find happiness in my imagination. . . . But you know," I'll say, looking askance towards the dark corner, "something seems to hinder seriously even this kind of search. It would seem to be so easy to look in the world of fantasy for that, which is ideal for you: select what you want, combine it any way you want, improve it and put it into desired constructions. But no, the selected will be inevitably corrupted by the undesirable, and the whole construction will fall apart with a crash. Here's a fresh example: I met a beautiful stranger; I idealized her, yet—suddenly attacked and violated her. And she, just imagine that, she was not insulted, but grinned diabolically."

The teacher poured himself another half a glass. He smelled it with disgust. It won't go down without water. He got up from the chair. The darkness swayed. A point appeared in its center. The darkness began to spin around the point. In a spiral. It was crawling into the point or the point was sucking up the darkness. He felt his way around the stove. The main thing is to walk straight, not to give in to the movement of the darkness. Otherwise you'll also start moving in a spiral. It would be interesting, though, to give in to the darkness, to start moving in a spiral, get sucked into the point and emerge in another world where absolutely everything is different. He poked his hand into a cold canister. Aha, on its top there should be a dipper. He groped around. The dipper came down with a bang. He got down on his knees and felt the floor. There's no dipper. As if earth swallowed it. He hit his head. The bench. Under the bench. Not there. Then where? I must think. The same dull, measured knocking, but, for some reason, much louder. He crawled cautiously towards the knocking. Something is sprinkling. Fine, sharp particles. He stuck his forehead into something wet. A stool. And a leaky faucet above. There is no basin underneath, and the drops, falling down, knock against the stool. He found a towel and put it on the stool. Now it's not knocking anymore. That's the way everything in life is. It's not a distant heart, but simply the drops from the faucet. A sober peasant approached the bull, looked at it, dragged a pole along, stuck it between the bull's legs, yanked the pole, and the bull fell down, like a statue. He had been dead for a long time, perhaps after the first strike. Aha, here's the dipper. He returned to the table, splashing out almost all the water. Poured the vodka into his mouth. Swallowing the vodka, he chased it with water. And began waiting for the ringing.

7

I'll step into the dark and the cool. It's quiet. And what is that lilac glow in front of me? Someone indistinct, surrounded by lilac-white aura, like a white cat seen in my childhood in a dark abandoned house, will touch my elbow and lead me towards the lilac glow.

Just a moment ago, I, a seventh-grader, was idling in front of the X-ray room. Seeing that the red *No Entrance* sign disappeared, I snuck into the narrow, black crack, got stuck in the velvet curtain and when I finally disentangled myself, I saw the lilac light in the darkness. I froze as if on the threshold of a house, in which a great magician lived. Barely breathing, I saw how a lilac table, a pile of lilac papers and a pale lilac nurse's cap appeared in the lilac aura. Something suddenly flooded all this, I heard a quick laugh, detected a faint smell of medicine, the smell of milky breathing, the smell of shiny, gorgeous hair, the smell of. . . . Only young pretty nurses smell like that. "And are we going to stand here long?" I heard her sarcastic voice. But I didn't move. I mumbled, "It's so dark here, I can't see a thing." Oh, you sly seventh-grader, sly as can be, you wanted to feel her warm hand on your cool body. She touched me; I happily shrunk away; tiny needles pricked my skin. Tenderly squeezing my elbow, she led me somewhere. Ah, how I loved these fleeting moments; she, mature and beautiful, warmly touching my shoulder, leads me into the lilac twilight.

"Excuse me," I'll ask, halting, "Do you have any European food?"

"Absolutely, sir. A large selection," the white and lilac cat will purr out.

I will look around. It'll seem to me there are people in the far, dark corner. I'll squint at them and they'll blow away.

"A booth, sir?" The cat will squint towards the same far corner.

Booths. . . . I love them for their refined loneliness; just you alone and a rosette of caviar, a sweaty carafe of vodka, the gentle birds of your imagination; the bird in front of you is an aristocratic lady from the past and the bird to your side—a country girl in a short, airy dress.

The cat and I will inspect the booths. Most of them appear empty, but above one partition a knot of hair is crowning an invisible woman. The knot is quivering. She's crying, or laughing, or talking. I'll finish the sketch of her interlocutor. A little mustache, bulging eyes, shiny black hair split from forehead to the back of the head by a narrow white streak of skin.

I'll choose the table, order a glass of vermouth and drink it the Russian way—greedily and in one gulp. I'll sprawl out. I'll listen to music; it'll quietly stream down from the ceiling, endless and heart-rending, and it'll bring to mind the snowstorm in the steppe, horses, and a coachman in love. On one side of the restaurant, a lilac bar will float along, like a bright lilac cloud. Among the fancy bottles, I'll notice one with double walls and a glass schooner inside.

The door of the restaurant will open. The blinding ray of sunlight will carry in silhouettes of a man and a girl; the particles of dust in the restaurant will become brighter and they will begin circling anxiously in front of the silhouettes. The door will close; it will become dark, and the headwaiter will slink by. The rustle of the girl's dress will intertwine with the heart-rending music.

The gentle rustle of your dress is like the rustle of the quiet fall, Pavlik, a friend of my youth, once breathed out, slowing down and stretching each sound of his poem. And what did he do to my soul, dissolved by aromatic Bessarabian wine, passionately loving every woman and loved by none in return! From that time on, the word *rustle* evokes in me a deep and wonderful sadness, pain at the roots of my hair and tears dripping into a glass of red wine.

The rustle will get stronger and it will now resemble the rustle of the leaves of the ancient tree; the silhouettes of the man and the girl will reach my table. I'll look intently into her indistinct face; she'll turn it towards me for a moment. I'll be choked and spun around by the space filled, as in the warm Southern night, with stars, music, somebody's breathing, whispers, lightning bugs, a woman's laughter, cicadas, soft splashing of the waves, the smoldering cigarette, the dark abyss of the luxuriant tree's shadow, a bench, and a couple flying into the abyss.

The man and the girl will sit down at the table in the left corner of my view. I'll turn away politely; my eyes will wander for a while and rest on the glass schooner in the bottle.

Under the glass sails, the glass owner of the glass hotel will be signing with a glass pen a pile of glass checks and he'll flash his glass teeth. "Oh, it's you, Mr. Donat," the words will start jumping, like glass beads. "We parted only yesterday, and I already am, hah-hah, a billionaire. My hotel, *Million Monkeys*, is one of the most popular hotels in the world. All the richest people of the earth want to stay in the hotel with such a name. They're opening their wallets even more willingly when they find out that the hotel is aboard a schooner. Finally, they go completely crazy and give me their last cent when they realize whither we are sailing. No, you'll die laughing when you see this crowd of people, rich yesterday and poor today, humbly floating down the course I'm charting." "You're charting the course?" I'll ask, incredulous. "Not for yourself, but for the entire crowd?" "Oh, it doesn't matter, Mr. Donat. A paradise is a paradise, what difference does it make who's charting the course thither." "Mr. Verma, you're mistaken; one paradise for all is hard to imagine. You are born and you're a ball rolling in a groove. You don't see its continuation; it is inextricably interwoven with countless other grooves, but only your groove will lead you to your paradise, if you're ever going to get there at all. Don't count on the crowd. You get a crowd when many balls are simultaneously rolling next to each other for some time. Don't count on love and friendship. They are nothing else, but two balls temporarily rolling next to each other. Sooner or later they'll diverge. We are alone from the day we are born. Like a train in the night, like the moon, like a leaf in a puddle, like a dead man, like me, like you. . . ." "Mr. Donat, you're a pessimist. I think that everything is wonderfully arranged. I became a billionaire. I'm sailing to paradise.

And, pardon my expression, I don't give a spit about
your grooves as long as they, hah-hah, aren't on a
woman." "Well, why not, Mr. Verma, you may be right;
women are worth everything. Listen, Verma, we know
each other, so let's drop the Misters and be friends. I'm
simply Donat and you're Verma. Without the Mister,
your name is like a wine. You're yellow, sweet, strong,
with a flavor of smoked nuts. I'm white, dry, and sour.
We are two bottles of different wines. Where is your glass,
let's have a toast; I'll drink you and you'll drink me. You
aren't such a bad wine, Verma. Listen, Verma, do you
see the table in the left corner of my view? Two people, a
heavy elderly man and a delicate trembling girl are sitting there in silence. Now look at the bar. That bottle
with double walls and a light brown drink confines a
great dream. Some eccentric, who has never fallen, never
hit himself against life, decided to encase his dream in a
double glass, and he strengthened it with a drink that all
people call strong, but as soon as they drink it, they become weak. Listen, Verma, doesn't it seem to you that
the table on the left and this bottle are, in some way,
astonishingly alike? That the man looks like the bottle
and the girl—like the schooner? Listen, Verma, let's drink
this stocky, aging man, and the dream will be mine."

The waiter will approach me.

"Sir, may I take your order?"

"Yes, more vermouth. What did those two order?"

He'll turn towards the table on the left, crowded with
pots and plates.

"Permit me, sir. Today, saab and memsa are eating
rice biryani, lady fingers, papadam, pickles, chutney,
rasam. . . ."

"Bring me the same," I'll interrupt the waiter.

"As you please. Sir, rasam too?"

"What?"

"Have you ever tried rasam?"

"I don't know. Maybe I did. Why, is it very common?"

"Very, sir."

"At least what does it look like?"

"It is, sir. . . . It resembles. . . . I don't know how to explain it. It is complex, tasty and bitter."

"What does the word *rasam* mean?"

"In Sanskrit, the word *rasa* means the juice of life or that, which feeds life."

"Well, interesting, what is it made of?"

"I don't remember the exact proportions, but for rasam you need dal, black pepper, garlic, cardamom seeds, fresh ginger, tamarind, asafoetida, a green tomato, salt, and a little branch of kerbela just picked off the tree. All this is cooked for a long time over a low heat.

"All right, rasam and the rest."

He'll nod with relief and run away. A complex, tasty and bitter dish. I would describe our life with exactly the same words.

A familiar rustle, from the quiet to the wild. The deafening rustle around me, as if I were in the depths of a tree-crown being torn apart by a hurricane.

Here is your little branch of kerbela; take it quickly, while it is next to you, for without it your paradise is impossible, I'll hear, or think that I hear.

Sudden silence. How nice it is when it's quiet. How nice it is when in the silence there's a soft clatter of dishes and heart-rending quiet music. I will quickly look at the girl. No, I was wrong. Not at me. The girl will look at her father. The father consists of the shaking nape framed at the bottom by curls, and a rounded stocky back. This nape. This back. I'll look with animosity at the barrier between me and the little branch of kerbela.

8

The teacher's room was dark like a grave. And the silence in the room was like the silence in a grave. And the mood in the room resembled the mood of those laying in a grave. And all these visions from the future resembled visions of the spirit that separated itself from the body and was hovering above. And only the square of the window in front of him, which looked as if the dark cloth of space had burned away in that one particular spot, only that burned-away square kept him from believing that he was in a grave.

He felt for the bottle and shook it. The dregs splashed softly. He started to move his hand along the table, looking for the glass. "Ah! Ah!" he moaned as if in a nightmare. His heart raced and his lungs turned into stone. How would you feel if, in total silence and darkness, almost believing that you were in a grave, you stuck your hand into a cold, slippery and decomposing dead body? The hand shot back; something fell on the floor, cracked, and rung, scattering around. That's the glass. And before that it was the lard. I'll finish what is left and go to sleep. Tomorrow is a holiday. I'll lie around.

Half asleep, when everything was spinning and he was falling down and flying up, the teacher saw someone approach him. He looked. Ah, it was his Natashenka. She was smiling at him with remorse. "It's all right," he whispered, "it's all right, my darling; it's all right, my little branch of kerbela." She laughed, flew away and instantly merged with the spinning of everything.

Ten Past Ten

Dressed too lightly for the arctic Nord-Ost, I continued staggering across the almost deserted center of the
southern city. Like most teenagers, I believed in the possibility of a miracle—an unknown girl rushing into my
arms. At an intersection, barely staying on my feet, I finally began to doubt whether it was worth continuing
to cross what I had already crossed many times. Above
my head, a branch of some delicate tree was in a panic.
As I raised my hand to comfort it, a taxi stopped next to
me. I peeked inside. The street lamp was no help. Its
insane swinging and dim light hindered my efforts to
define more precisely a marvelous, feminine figure in
the depths of the dark cab. As for the second passenger,
looking like an Armenian, well, I was not interested in
him.

"Where to?" the taxi driver shouted to me.

"Where are you going?" I asked, feigning interest.

"To the new suburb. Where do you want to go?"

I had no idea and fell silent. The taxi driver was patient.

"How much to go there?" I asked just in case.

"I won't skin you alive. Come on in!"

I got in a taxi I did not need and I headed for a suburb
to which I did not need to go. Only the presence of the
girl and the beastly cold outside could have justified this
absurd behavior. I wanted to look at the girl who was
sitting behind me, but that would have forced me to turn
around and make contact with the eyes of the Armenian. Who knows, perhaps he was not her traveling com-

panion, but just a fellow traveler. Not about to take any chances, I sat still for the time being and did not turn around. The heater in the taxi worked well and I began to warm up blissfully.

The car leaped out of the center of the city and ran down the shore of the bay. The Nord-Ost tried to push us off the road, to overturn us, or lift us in the air. It turned the tidal spray into a gusting downpour that froze on every surface. The windshield-wipers somehow defended their territory on the glass, but the rest of the car and everything around it was enveloped in a crust of ice rising in fantastic ice formations and descending into icicles of sinister sizes. The road reflected the car's lights like a river. The driver did not race, but, oh, how I wished he would slow down!

A gigantic sheet of ice hit the car and swept us to the side of the road. The driver stepped on the brake and the car skidded. Turning the steering wheel furiously, like a racer on the serpentine of a mountain road, the driver miraculously managed to regain control of the cab. We were all shaken. Everybody lit a cigarette. Everybody, that is, except me.

"We've got a flock of swans in the estuary now," the taxi driver said, trying to start a conversation. He was a thin man with a face weathered by the wind and creased by wrinkles. He sported a perpetual brownish tan—not for naught was he a taxi driver in a southern city.

"Swans in the estuary?" the Armenian asked, surprised. "Don't they live in fresh water? Water in the estuary is horribly salty. How many are there?"

"A hundred, perhaps half a hundred. No way to count them. They don't stay in one place, you know."

"They'll get covered with ice and freeze to death," said the Armenian. "Have you noticed how many pochards wash out on the shore after weather like this?"

"They'll die all right," nodded the driver. "Wind like this can turn tankers over and wash them ashore, so how can such tiny creatures survive?"

I was listening, wondering about the swans, looking through the windshield-wipers at the road, and thinking of what to do next. On the other hand, what difference did it make? The main thing was that I was warm. As for the girl behind me. . . . O.K. Let this girl remain a vague and lovely silhouette inside a warm, dark iron capsule flying through an ice-cold hurricane, moving dangerously along the icy river-like road, under a shower of shattered sea spray.

"Drop me off at the fork," I said suddenly.

The taxi driver obviously did not hear me right, for he did not react at all. Only the car slipped a little. I felt on the back of my head the huge question of the Armenian.

"At the fork," I said louder.

"Take a leak, or what?" the driver asked.

The Armenian laughed eagerly.

"No, I just need to get out there."

"Why? There is nothing at all there. The empty steppe; nothing else. Aren't you from here, or what? What do you want?"

The driver turned to the Armenian.

"You live here, don't you? Tell him something."

"Hey, he's not a child," said the Armenian. "If that's what he wants, let him out."

"Listen, young man," said the taxi driver. "Let me explain it to you once more. The fork is in the middle of nowhere. Nothing, but the empty shore and the barren steppe there. In a wind and cold like this, you are looking at something like minus twenty-five. You'll croak, you understand? Besides, it's about three kilometers to the nearest houses. You'll die from the cold, I'm telling you. If you had a fur coat, a hat, and warm boots, I would . . . even then I would object. Take a look at your clothes. All you got on is that thin raincoat? Where the devil are you going, anyway?"

"To the estuary," I said.

The driver whistled.

"So, it's those swans! Well, why don't you wait 'til morning? Take a look around you. It's pitch dark. You won't see a damn thing."

"Why are you arguing with him?" asked the Armenian. "Don't you see he's crazy? Let him out!"

The fork appeared. The taxi driver slowed down. I looked at him and understood that he wasn't about to stop, but was ready to turn towards the suburb. He agreed with the Armenian that I was crazy, but he didn't want me to die.

"Here!" I said sharply.

The driver pushed my money aside, turned away and looked at the frozen glass as I was getting out. I was now in the grip of the Nord-Ost. I didn't follow the red disappearing lights of the car with my eyes. It was so piercingly cold that I started to run as fast as I could. Soon I slipped on the sleet, fell down, jumped up, and began running more cautiously. I fell again, this time pushed by a wind gust. Now I hurt myself quite badly. While I was lying, massaging my knee, the next blast blew me onto the side of the road.

Nevertheless, not everything tried to stop me. For instance, the border patrol's projectors suddenly decided to help me. Aimed at the clouds, they flared up somewhere in the hills and frantically rushed about. It seemed as if the clouds from abroad were flying too fast over industrial and military secrets of my eternally suspicious fatherland and alarmed the border guards. A part of the reflected light of the projectors fell conveniently to my feet. At that moment I already knew that I wouldn't be able to reach the estuary and if, for some miraculous reason, I did manage to get there, I would become dangerously ill. I also knew that after reaching the estuary I would not be able to see anything in the darkness. Even the clouds reflecting the rays of the border projectors would not help me there.

Running did not help me either. I was freezing and moving ahead ever more slowly. My hands turned into slabs of ice. I kept this ice under my armpits for some time. Then, with my icy hands, I tried to warm up the piece of ice that my face had become. Turning often away from the wind and moving towards the estuary backward, I looked at the harbor lights, which resembled the stars on the horizon. I wished I could return to the fork, but it was so far to go back that both going forward or back meant the same thing—a stiff lying on a road rarely traveled in winter.

At one moment, turning away from the wind, I saw a dancing light in the distance. I realized that these were headlights, that a car was catching up with me. Someone else, besides me, decided to look at the swans, I thought indifferently. The car caught up with me and stopped.

"Hey, don't be a fool, get in," called a voice I recognized as the taxi driver's.

I got inside. Somehow.

Strange things were going on while I was sick with pneumonia. For instance, when from the heights of the spare pillow I stared for a long time at my legs, deformed by the thick blanket, they would begin to grow longer. They would grow until they reached the wall, and then the wall would obediently move aside. If I said, "My legs are on the street," the legs would easily penetrate the wall, extend through the bushes across the entire yard, screw themselves into the cracks between the boards in the fence, and barricade the sidewalk. Passersby would go around the legs or jump over them. If I 'd stretch my legs even farther, they would barricade the entire street. The cars would stop and honk. Then the drivers would knock on our gate and ask me to remove the legs.

When the legs could no longer amuse me, I would turn on my side and look either at the wall or at the bedside table. After looking at the wall for a long time, I would hear the plaster rustle in my ears, a stony aftertaste would appear in my mouth, and a stony ache would fill my eyes and my nose. I would also hear the stony banging of the dishes in the kitchen, the stony ticking of the alarm clock, and the stony barking of the dogs in the street.

Bored with the stony world, I would turn to face the bedside table and amuse myself with the alarm clock; I watched the movement of its minute hand. During the first days of my illness, I did not notice anything abnormal. It is true that the minute hand of the alarm clock puzzled me when its smooth running changed into unpredictable jumps, sometimes by several notches, sometimes by a quarter of the circle, and sometimes by God only knows how much. Even worse were the terrifying jumps in the opposite direction. Nevertheless, I was able to unravel all these scary knots of time without difficulty. I realized I had been either lost in deep thought or napping, or simply forgot to wind the clock.

One evening, I could not fall asleep. My stepfather's lips were making splashing sounds, and my mother was puffing quietly. In front of me was the clock's face, delicately lit by the full, anxious moon. It was five after ten. I followed the minute hand. Exhaustingly slowly, but smoothly, it was moving in the right direction.

At ten past ten, the hands of the alarm clock suddenly became longer, bent, grew white feathers, flapped up and down, and into the spherical sky flew a large gracious bird. Its neck vibrated like a released arrow, its pink eyes sparkled, and its wings mightily chopped the air. Watching the rhythmic movements of the wings, I must have dozed off. Then, with a shudder, I opened my eyes and saw an unfamiliar ceiling. It was covered with the water-spots left after old rains and by scabs of deteriorating whitewash. I sat up and looked around carefully.

My narrow iron bed stood in a spacious single room that was lit too brightly. The sun was bursting unhindered through the slanted gaping window. The dusty pieces of the windowpane lay scattered around the dirty floor. The same sun, like an insatiable murderer-sadist, kept stabbing the boards of the rickety walls with thousands of knives made of golden dust. Golden ray-spears, ray-swords, and ray-maces stuck out from the wall that faced the sun. Close to the window, I saw a table, a stool, and an abandoned rusty bucket. Behind the gaping window unfolded the yellow steppe and a strip of water as calm as a mirror. The door looked as if it had broken loose from its hinges and had begun to fall, but reconsidered. Everything around the bed was wrapped in many years of heavy cobwebs and frosted with a thick layer of dust.

I got up and approached the window. Submerged to their waist in water, naked young women slowly wandered about the estuary. Their white loose hair fluttered and flapped in the wind. To see them better, I tried to move my head into the gaping window frame, but my forehead knocked against something. I peered at this *something*, stretched my hand out, and my palm rested on a hard invisible coolness. I pushed my forehead against the coolness and watched one of the girls walk straight in my direction. The water was slowly receding and the girl's nakedness kept increasing. Our glances met and she stopped. I walked across the room from the window to the door and pushed it to make it fall on the yellow grasses, but for some reason the door did not budge. Using my shoulder, I slammed against the door. The shoulder began to hurt, but the door was still standing. I broke off a board in the wall, stuck it in between the door and the frame, and pushed. The board broke easily. I shouted something, but the result of my cry was an unintelligible moan. . . .

Mother was shaking me by my shoulder. The moon had already abandoned the alarm clock that was hardly visible in the darkness. I turned my face to the wall. Mother kissed me on the back of my head, sighed, and returned to bed; I could hear the springs squeak. The dogs were not barking, and I was not asleep. Then, as usual, everything turned into stone.

In the morning, at five past ten, I was staring at the clock, waiting. The minute hand moved to ten past ten, but nothing interesting happened. Sick, I was impatiently waiting for the night, for the late ten past ten. At ten in the evening, everybody went to bed. The moon was not touching the alarm-clock. After twenty-four hours of turning and complicated wanderings around the heavens, not only the moon, but also the entire solar system shifted towards the wall by my feet. Trying hard not to make noise, I moved the bedside table to the spot where the moon could touch the clock. This took me exactly seven minutes. With a commanding glance, I sped the minute hand up.

At ten past ten, the hands of the clock flinched, bent gently, and a large bird flew into the sky. I already knew it was a swan. Again, its neck was vibrating like a released arrow, the moon gleamed in its eyes like blood, and the wings were cutting the air with a wail. The flight of the changeling-swan stirred my senses. Below the swan, I saw the stormy sea, the shore and the triangle of the estuary. The swan folded its wings, turned over, and with its beak pointing towards the water, dropped like a heavy stone into the triangular mirror that reflected nothing. . . .

The alarm-clock, deserted by the moon, tick-tocked like a phantom. Stepfather was snoring. Mother was quiet. The dog was confessing to the moon. The night followed its ordinary course; it kept alternating the petrifaction and pneumonia, the bitter medicine and milk with honey, deep sleep and exhausting insomnia. The new morning brought more medicine; a long urination into the bucket, which robbed me of the remaining night warmth; the breakfast of the stove that chewed the wood with a crackle; the smell of smoke; gradual warming up of our little house; the ringing of dishes, and, finally, my breakfast—fresh porridge and yesterday's cutlets swallowed without appetite.

The next night, there was no moon; the clouds did something to the planet before they started pouring on it a gentle, sad, and long-lasting rain. I had to convince my parents that at night I needed a little light, that perhaps a lamp left on in the kitchen would suffice. "The nightmares are tormenting me," I complained in a feeble voice, "and when I wake up in the Egyptian darkness I am not sure whether I am awake or the nightmare continues." My stepfather, without hiding his displeasure, adjusted the narrow shafts of light coming through the doors from the kitchen to the bedroom, "so that your stupid and crazy games do not blind me during the night." Somehow, the light from the kitchen managed to drag itself through the tight cracks in the doors and through the room between them. It died on the beds and in the corners, but it survived on the clock's face.

At ten past ten, I mounted the swan; however, we did not make it to the estuary. Above some tiny settlement, the swan slowed down its flight, descended, shook me off to the ground and disappeared in the darkness. I found myself in a room with a counter. A man approached me; he was the manager of this hotel. He was a mountain of a man with a huge, tired head. At first I thought he was naked, but he was naked before he approached me. He was sleeping with his wife, naked as usual, but when I took a closer look at him he was already wrapping himself in a thick bathrobe and hiding his feet in warm slippers.

"Do you have money?" he asked me.

Surprisingly, I understood him perfectly, even though he asked in a foreign language. I did not plan to stay in this hotel (it seemed to me that I already had accommodations). Anyway, I knew nothing about money.

"That's what I thought," nodded the mountain. It put its elbows on the counter and looked beyond me in the way the martyrs do.

There, where the mountain looked, a lamp was swinging beyond the window, a tree branch was scratching, and the rain was drizzling.

"Why did you come to this dump?"

I did not know that either, but I had to give him an answer.

"Fate brought me here," I said.

Apparently, this answer satisfied him, although the exhaustion on his face did not diminish, but rather increased. Evidently, my answer hit the target, some tormenting target; maybe it was somehow connected to the exhaustion torturing his face.

"Perhaps," he started, looking at the bad weather and drawing energy from the lamp swinging madly outside; without realizing it, the manager drew energy for his enormous body from the wind, so far sufficiently strong to prevent his complete exhaustion. "Perhaps this is a new trend—to travel around the world without a wallet. However bizarre it is, but—so be it. So be it!" he shouted in a deafening voice, signifying that he did not approve of it at all.

"I almost got used to it," he continued with a voice of a man who had been hanging upside down for a long time, but who did not lose hope that somehow his life would change for the better. "But I can't understand at all what foreigners with empty pockets are doing in our god-forsaken fishing village that has no museums, no interesting crafts, not even any exceptional rocks. Why come to a boring place where flora consists only of grass resembling razor blades and dirty disheveled bushes, and fauna of lethargic fish and noisy obnoxious sea-gulls? What else can I say," he said with a wave of his hand, while his body, suspended by his legs, swung and started to turn around slowly. "Nobody here was even born with a third eye, a tail, a sixth finger, a criminal mind or anything uncommon that would make him stand out from the crowd reeking of fish. . . ."

I was silent. I tried to understand why, indeed, those penniless foreigners kept coming to this hole, and why I came here as well. A fisherman fishes in a god-forsaken bay, dries and inspects his nets, throws little fish to his cat or to a sea-gull (if he does not have a cat), and suddenly a foreigner appears. He does not look at anything because there is nothing to look at and he does not buy anything because he has no money; instead, he just rests on a rock and simply sits there, confusing the fisherman with his looking.

An exhausted smile saddened the slowly-rotating profile that was turning into a disheveled nape.

"And yet, that's not true," the manager muttered through his sadly bent lips. "We do have one thing worthy of notice—our strong, endless winds. Let me be more specific—our accursed winds."

"I am familiar with that," I nodded with joy. "You know, I also live in a city with accursed winds."

"Then we do understand each other," he agreed with his smiling nape; yet, I only imagined that smile, I doubt that he ever smiled.

"By the way," I asked to support the revolving conversation, "do you really see many foreigners here?"

"Too many for my depressed point of view. And none of them, I should repeat, has any money or possessions, and no one knows why they come here."

Suddenly, the house shook and thundered as if it had been hit by an earthquake. Actually, the host turned himself upside down and jumped on the floor. His awakened wife also turned calmly in bed and immediately went back to sleep; she was used to various inconveniences related to her husband's size.

He scratched his cheeks absentmindedly—as noisily as if he were running an iron brush over iron—and realized that he had not shaved for a long time. With a melancholic look, he went behind the counter and began to pull all the available handles and open everything that could be opened. The process ended when he discovered the straight-edged razor (precisely like the one my stepfather had), a piece of soap in a plastic cup, and the dried-up shaving brush. He splashed into the cup some water and managed to whip up some foam.

"Excuse me, wouldn't you happen to have a belt on you?" he asked, suddenly realizing he was not wearing a leather belt, but had on a belt used to tie bathrobes.

Of course, I obliged. However, he did not like my belt because it was not made of leather. Unable to hide his disappointment, he handed the belt back to me and at the same time looked at my unimpressive shoes.

"Maybe your shoes have leather soles?"

I did not know that either, but I handed him one shoe. He examined its sole, tapped at it with his fingers, flicked off a few pieces of dirt, rubbed it with his sleeve, licked it, and kept watching how the sole absorbed the saliva. Apparently, it absorbed it in a way only leather can. The corners of his lips rose about one millimeter.

"I'll tell you straight; I am astounded. Your shoes are lousy, but the leather is acceptable."

He cleared his throat, ran his thumb across the razor, and began to sharpen it. I knew from my stepfather's routine what it meant to sharpen the razor properly. The process would take too long to stand and wait for the shoe. So, with eyes fixed on the rhythmically flashing blade, I went to the armchair and, seated comfortably, continued to watch the flashes. I must have fallen asleep because the next thing I saw was a cleanly shaven man in pants and an ironed shirt. Noticing that I opened my eyes, he said, "Catch!" and threw the shoe to me. Only when the shoe hit my outstretched hands and jumped somewhere to the side, did I assume that this was the hotel manager. My assumption was immediately confirmed by the dejected expression, exaggerated earlier by the unattended stubble on his face. Clearly, the causes of dejection are hidden so deep under the skin that some country probably has a saying: *Dejection is not a beard; it cannot be shaven off*. I went on all fours behind an old heavy sofa to fish out my lousy shoe that managed to sharpen the razor. However, just as I sat down to put the shoe on, the voice with pre-shaving intonations (the voice is not a beard either; it also cannot be shaven off) continued with dejected intimacy:

"But even more strange is that no arriving foreigners stay in the village even one day. They loiter here, in the office, without money and without reason, and if I leave them just for a few minutes, when I come back they are gone."

He approached me, bent over, and said into my ear, "There are even stranger things. The strangest of them is that no one ever comes back!"

He recoiled and dropped to his knees. His action rocked the entire house; somewhere below, a heavy chandelier fell down with a thunderous crash. He threw his hands towards me. His exhausted face proved capable of even greater suffering. He lamented in an imploring whisper and whispered a martyr's lament.

"Sir," he said, "You are one of those people. I beg you! Do you have a mother? Do you believe in God? What do you believe in? What is the holiest thing for you? In the name of what is most sacred to you, tell me why did you come here?"

It was painful to look at him. I would have been glad to admit anything to lessen his suffering. I wished he'd given me a clue as to what I needed to say and how I needed to say it. I remembered he was satisfied with my first answer and I said with greatest sincerity:

"Fate, Sir, brought me here. Fate."

He sat on the armchair, the chair, and the sofa—he was a very wide man.

"Nothing's sacred to you," he moved his emaciated tongue.

We sat listening to the sounds of the rain. I was not in a hurry to get anywhere. And yet, my unexplained presence continued to torment him. He jumped up again, hovered over me and began to change the position of his hands. He placed them in his pockets, folded them on his chest, dropped them to his stomach and inter-

twined the fingers, threw them behind his back, lowered them completely, that is, he let them dangle around
his hips, and there he nervously collected and spilled
his mighty fists. Finally, he returned his hands to his
pockets.

"I have not been here long," he began in an almost
conciliatory voice. "Only three years. Before me, there
was no hotel here at all. Even so, you see for yourself
that nobody needs this hotel. Two pitiful rooms, vacant
all the time. . . . I make my money only on the restaurant. And what kind of money is that? Barely enough to
cover my expenses. Why, you would ask, did I drag
myself to do business in this hole? I did not come here to
do business. I was traveling along the shore. You know,
I used to enjoy a slow and painstaking progress along
the coastline. I took all kinds of risks to remain as close
as possible to the salt water. I had a dream; I wanted to
copy the complex outlines of the existing continents with
the movement of my amazingly conspicuous body, using it like a thick marker. . . . And how about you?" he
asked just to shake me up. "Do you like traveling?"
He did the right thing; I was falling asleep. It was,
after all, the middle of the night. I came alive, nodded,
and smiled. It appeared I had managed to satisfy him.
"And so, traveling along the shore to achieve the
dream of my life, I kept so close to the ocean waves that
one late evening, in the thick fog, I did not notice a preci-
pice. In short, I fell down God knows where. Overloaded
as usual, we (my car and I) were falling down fast and
almost endlessly; we were plunging to be squashed into
an example of bloodstained progress. During that fall, I
had enough time to recollect all the events of my life, to

say good-bye to my family, friends, and even to those whom I had never met. I also had time (if only in my head) to put my affairs in eternal order. On the bottom of that everlasting fall, we suddenly met not an executioner, masquerading as a rock, but a wise and impartial ocean laughing under his gray mustache. While the car was moving here and there, mainly in the direction of the bottom, I managed to get out through the window in a manner not very elegant, but clearly perfectly appropriate under the circumstances. I swam to the shore, shook the water off, undressed, wrung out all my clothes, and put them back on, even though they were still wet. First, I grieved for a while over the loss of my maps, on which very diligently I had outlined with markers my intricate route, the route that agreed as precisely as possible with the outlines of the lands and oceans. In the second place, I grieved over the loss of my documents, money, and a case of *Wild Turkey* that was my favorite consolation in the absence of human life. . . ."

"And you," he asked me point-blank, "what do you think of *Wild Turkey*?"

Again, he yanked me out of some dream. "Well, what's your answer?" he asked with hostility after an adequate wait.

"I like it, yes, I like it," I said at last. "But I don't recall the exact taste. I ate some a long time ago."

"It's whiskey," he said quietly. His face showed abhorrence. Oh, how he hated me for my lies, for my general ignorance, for my presence, and even for my inevitable future absence.

He shuddered from loathing, came to himself, and continued his story.

"In the third place, but not in the last, I grieved over the loss of my poor jeep, which, with great strain but loyally, used to transport my oversized body. For a while I grieved over some other things; then I climbed the nearest rock and saw a small light in the distance. Without delay, I went in its direction. That night was almost like this one. At the same time, it was strikingly different, if only because there was no hotel here. Thoroughly wet, cold, and hungry, like an orphan or a homeless person, I wandered in the cold rain, through the puddles, from house to house. Did I knock on the doors? You bet, I did. I knocked on all the doors I saw. I will not hide the fact that all of them opened. Not right away, but all of them did open. The fishermen, joined by their wives and children, sleepily stared at my huge, wet body. Their not completely awakened bodies and their ramshackle homes aggressively attacked me with assorted smells of fish: raw, boiled, smoked, fried, fresh, and even spoiled a year before. My hunger was fighting with nausea and it was losing this brutal battle. I did not know their language then, but with the help of gestures I was denying that I intended to rob them, kill them, or violate their women. Categorically, but insincerely, I also denied the truth, that is, I was trying to convince them that I was neither hungry, nor cold.

"Oh no, folks," I kept assuring them, jerking my limbs like a stringed-up marionette, mercilessly dipped in the cold ocean and then left hanging in the wind under a cold foreign rain. "No, I don't need your fish or your beds. What I want is a space on your hard floor, a space the size of my coiled up body (it's huge, of course, but do not be frightened; my wandering life taught me very well how to coil up in any space that was forced upon me). What I want is a roof over my body, for no longer than until the early dawn."

I pointed my finger at their roofs, but they imagined that I poked it into the sky. I don't think I looked like a missionary; yet, the fishermen were sure I had arrived to convert them without their knowledge to some other faith. They smiled with a frown, or frowned with a smile; they shoved me into the rain, turned off the lights, and went to bed. That night has opened my eyes to the true nature of all human beings, and since that time, I have been seized with an endless and boundless depression. Having lost in the ocean depths everything that enabled me to copy the capricious outlines of the land masses and oceans, and having turned into a foreign vagabond of suspiciously large dimensions, I made a difficult deci-sion—to stay here for the time being. Three years have gone by. I am still here. I have a feeling I'll die here, as well."

He started crying. I did not know how to help him. I myself needed help, a roof over my coiled-up body. Meanwhile, he kept shedding crocodile tears. I ran into a man who terribly misjudged people during one rough night of his life. Others suffer and become kinder. But this man was different; he became embittered and woke up a beast inside him.

"Well, here you have it," he said, having dried his eyes. "You refused to help me with the smallest thing— you didn't give me an answer why you came here. For that, excuse me, I will refuse you also. Be so kind as to get out. I want to go to bed."

Urging me with his shoulder, that is, rudely and even painfully initiating bodily contact with me, the scoun-drel was able to inject into me an excess of his personal cosmic dejection; and thanks to this, his mood seemed to improve. He was too large for any kind of objections.

I went out to face the bad weather and my own problems. It turned out that I threw off my sheet, and the house cooled considerably at night. I don't remember whether the dogs were barking, but the alarm-clock tic-tocked, as always, and its every tick and every tock underlined the separate moments of the present receding into the past.

Now I was waiting for ten past ten as a girl waits for her first love, a boy for the death of his stepfather, an old woman for the death of her senile, disgraceful husband, and an old man for his last love. Let's not get confused by counting days, rummaging in some chronology and juggling a handful of specific hours or even worse—minutes. We are recalling general blows and caresses instead of the date and exact time of someone hitting us in the face or caressing the hair on the back of our head in a telephone booth. (To be more precise, before this serious illness, I did not yet have a chance to experience the crowding of telephone booths by three participants: him, her and the telephone, which somehow made the telephone completely superfluous. However, once or twice, I did watch similar group encounters from a distance, and I fantasized about their female participants). But let's not get baffled by all the unnecessary details. Better, let's recall what was happening and what I felt during the last days of my illness, after the hands of the alarm-clock created out of the general chaos twenty-two hours, ten minutes, and zero-zero seconds of city time.

The old house, as it turned out, did not flash and disappear like a face in a crowd or like everything else that is able to flash and disappear. The old house, with a view of the steppe and the estuary, became my prison, continually fanned by strong winds. From there, I could escape only to my real life. Obviously, I broke some important law, I committed some crime; someone put me on trial somewhere, and from time to time, at ten past ten, the swan would become a servant of the broken law and transport me to the old house, which perhaps was a prison for especially dangerous criminals.

Once, as I was watching the girls, I noticed out of the corner of my eye some other movement. Along the shore of the estuary, two monsters were walking in my direction, barely managing to carry on their shoulders a huge bundle, tightly wrapped with a rope. The clothing of the monsters was ordinary, but their hands and heads were terrifying. All the exposed parts of their bodies were covered with tangled fur, tumors, scabs, and skin diseases. Of course, one could relish such fine points as the monsters' gaping nostrils turned inside out and bubbling with puss and snot, warts of living frogs' heads on their faces and necks, deep sores swarming with worms and cockroaches, fangs, resembling rotten bones, and bobcats' yellow eyes, set so closely to each other that they continuously seemed to merge or separate, and if one wanted to describe their expression, it would have been easier to describe death.

However, we have no time for relishing all the fine points—the monsters noticed me. They stopped, discussed something, threw the bundle down on the yellow grass and began walking straight towards me. The wind unfolded the sackcloth covering the bundle, and from there, the glassy eyes of the hotel manager stared at the departing backs of the monsters and, at the same time, at me.

I should have yelled into the darkness of the night where my mother and my stepfather were; but for some reason, it did not happen. Instead, I ran to the closest corner, pinned myself against the wall and waited for the worst. I had only one ray of hope: since I knew I could not get out of the house, I hoped it was also impossible to get in. Even I did not get inside; I have always found myself in this house the way we all find ourselves in life—that is, only God knows how and why.

Someone loudly and energetically knocked on the door. I did not answer. The door opened. The head of a completely normal man appeared in the crack. He saw me in the corner, and asked in a workman's voice,

"You're in charge here, or what? Where do you want him, this son of a bitch? Outside by the wall, or inside?"

The second head pushed in through the doorway; it was also normal in appearance. In response to my silence, it went berserk.

"Why are you asking him? He is an idiot, don't you see? Where we dumped the corpse, it should stay. Fuck him, this moron! Let's have a swim. That son of a bitch broke my shoulders."

"Yep, it would be great to take a swim," agreed the first. "Hey, we forgot. How about the money? Did anyone leave you money for us?"

"No," I was finally able to answer. "Nobody left me anything."

"What do you mean nobody left you anything?" Both of them were stupefied.

I spread my hands to show I knew nothing.

"Should I beat his mug up?" asked one, picturing the pleasures of the beating with a smile learned in prisons.

"You bet," the second also smiled, and his smile came from the dungeons.

Anticipating an interesting mug-beating, the former and the future criminals moved towards me, wickedly swinging their bodies. Holding a wet cigarette in his lips twisted with disgust on my account, one of them puffed smoke in my face and then lifted above my head something dark, blurry, and filling half of the sky. . . .

The clouds clearly promised rain. Not to get my clothes soaked, I began to undress frantically. I was in a hurry to free myself from my foreign clothes full of buttons, zippers, and belts. My boxers turned out to be old and faded, and had a hole in the seat. I was going to throw them away long ago, so I tossed them aside with relief and gathered the rest of my clothes into a bundle.

It seemed to be late at night; but perhaps, I thought, it was not wise to be naked in the middle of this inhabited settlement. The boats of the fishermen often lingered and returned with their catch late at night, and sometimes even at dawn, especially on such windy days. The women who met the fishermen could easily stumble upon me, disguised as a naked foreigner. Undoubtedly, they would call the police. The police officer with a sleepy face would demand that I explain everything in local language. I would concentrate on their language and I would politely explain that I arrived quite recently and did not learn their laws yet. The policeman would ask for my documents. I would look for them in vain on my naked body. The policeman would lazily handcuff me, take me to the police station, lock me in the room they called a prison, and after the holidays, they would put me on trial. While this possible scenario was unfolding in my head, I was anxiously watching how two shadows, jerking like two boas, were creeping towards my own shadow. I turned around. Two men approached me. One of them took me by my elbow.

"Come with us," he said in a familiar voice.

I recognized the shadows; these were the monsters pretending to be workmen. I yanked my elbow and started to run. The sticky mud in the puddles was interfering with my escape. I was afraid the bundle with my clothes would plop from under my arm into the mud. I screamed. The hotel door opened, and the huge head came out. I understood: the manager was not dead yet; the pursuing monsters would kill him soon. He quickly started locking the door with the heavy outside latch, because he wanted the monsters to kill *me*. He openheartedly told me the story of almost his entire life, and I refused to answer just one question honestly. Miraculously, I managed to push his huge body away, broke the latch off, and locked myself inside the hotel. From the other side of the door, I heard sounds of heavy blows; the monsters were smashing the hotel manager's body and his skull. The latter crunched like an overripe melon; most likely, the attackers were using stones. I was not sorry they were killing him. This was his fate.

The naked girl from the estuary was dancing on a small stage. Here, one had to dance naked. I wanted to undress quickly, but I noticed I was already undressed. I had nothing under my arms; I must have dropped my clothes in the mud. I jumped in the direction of the stage. Stretching my leg as far as I could, I was able to extend my jump until I was right next to the girl. During my flight I was slightly afraid that I would not be able to land in time, that I would hit her or that I'd fall, that is, disappoint her in some way. Nevertheless, everything turned out just great. I took her by the hand and locked our fingers. Sweet bubbles appeared on the surface of my skin. She pressed herself to my entire body. I exploded and started pulsating.

The film of events broke off. I did not stomp my feet, whistle, or yell, "Make soap out of the projectionist." I sent him to a nice Black Sea resort, invented for him a meeting with an interesting woman, and then relaxed on my other side, thinking about the pleasant event that had happened to me in the mystical world existing beyond ten past ten.

One night, when I was in that world again, I heard through the wind a strange sound. Was it a teaspoon quietly jingling in a cup of tea? I glanced at the table next to the window, abruptly sat up in the bed, and got the wonderful feeling that I was a worthy man. Let me explain what is a worthy man; it is a man worthy of women.

A worthy man meets a woman in the foyer of some wealthy house. The host says, "Oh, yes, you don't know each other. Marcello, mon ami, let me introduce signorina Lucia Paolini. . . ." The passions flare. Having lost their heads, that same night the couple gets lost in the bed of his country villa. In the morning the wind awakens the girl. Without getting dressed, she quietly gets up and prepares breakfast for two. Looking in the window and listening to the wind, she is quietly eating her breakfast and accidentally makes a teaspoon jingle in her cup.

Now, he became I; I was a worthy man. I was looking at the beautiful naked girl sitting by the window, a steaming cup in her hand, and the breakfast on the table. I folded my hands on my chest, which was sun-tanned, muscular, and hairy. My hands were not much worse. I smiled like a man in the commercial advertising electric razors. The man stands in front of the mirror and impassively examines his sun-tanned face with a willfully divided chin and stern lines around his mouth. He is neither upset nor overjoyed by the dark, nightly growth. Calmly, he takes the electric razor, turns it on with his thumb, and then confidently slides the razor down his face. The cleanly shaven strip resembles the path left by a harvesting machine in a wheat field. The man's hard lips move; what can he do if so many ladies get so excited by his cleanly shaven cheeks?

"Hunger breaks heavy walls," I said without thinking about the meaning of my words because worthy men say everything carelessly and spontaneously.

She turned in my direction and smiled. I imperiously patted my hand on the bed. She came closer, sat on the edge. I put my muscular hand on her waspy waist. To my surprise, my hand became a stupid semicircle surrounding emptiness. She was already standing at the door. I showed a slight surprise and, somersaulting like a gymnast, nailed myself to the dusty floor. In this primary human position, I felt one personal item in its most elevated form. The girl blushed, lowered her eyes, and became even more beautiful. She made a sign to follow her and effortlessly pushed the door. The door fell flat on the grass. She started walking towards the estuary. Her firm buttocks began to wiggle in an indescribably wonderful way.

We (the worthy man and I) set out to follow the girl's
buttocks with the passion of a dog following a bone. We
knew the water in the estuary was blissful. Apparently,
the girl was proposing to combine the bliss of the water
with the bliss of uniting our naked bodies. We licked our
lips and increased our steps. She was already walking
across the blissful water, a mirror in front of her and the
shattered shards behind. We could not control ourselves;
we started to run. Like muscular dolphins, we jumped
into the slivers of the blissful broken water, into the bliss
the girl offered us. Hearing the tumultuous splashes of
the chase, she looked behind, smiled, kicked her legs,
and began to run. She was running and sinking. Her
arms detached from her hips, floated up to her shoulders like the wings of an airplane, rose a little higher,
flapped, and suddenly—we trembled—froze at exactly
ten past ten. We already knew what would happen next,
and we ended our chase, disappointed. The worthy man
blew up and vanished into the air.

Alone with the girl, I watched how at ten past ten her
arms grew white feathers, how she quickly turned into
a swan, how the strong wings flapped, how the swan
separated itself from the water, and how it flew into the
open sky. I was left with what is left to all people who
accompany somebody to the train station: they turn
around and walk quietly, feeling cheated and sad. I
turned to go back to the old house, but I could not pull
my leg out. I—who knew this estuary so well, who knew
its treacherous sticky bottom—I was stuck in it. She had
lured me out of the house to drown me!

Before the water reached my nostrils, I tried to fill the
last moments of my life as actively as possible with all
sorts of drowning-man's rubbish: jerking, splashing,

shouting, bugging my eyes out, disfiguring my face in terror, cursing all girls in the world, crying, and, finally, making bubbles.

I died and was born again—as a youth, not completely cured yet, but slowly beginning to recover.

A Ceiling
with Lizards

Some will say he was a good fellow; others will say he was a scoundrel. Both this and that will be false.

M. Lermontov. A Hero of Our Time

Even though the pedestrian encircled himself with the waterfall, he still resembled an umbrella attached for some reason to a mop just pulled out of a bucket. Through the wall of water he assured me and the driver that we were not wandering through the night jungle, but that we were actually in a village.

Encouraged, we continued driving or floating through shallow winding streets. Occasionally, in the tropical vegetation on both sides of those streets, we were able to discern isolated mansions. Distorted by the window panes of the car, they looked like hotels, but in each instance turned out not to be.

The heavens took pity on us again and sent us another man who, without an umbrella and without any apparent reason, stood in the middle of the flooded street. He opened his mouth to answer our question whether there was any hotel in the vicinity, but his mouth flooded instantly. Shaking from the cough, he pointed with his hand in the direction of a particular house.

We rang the bell to that potential overnight stay. A sleepy man came out. He turned out to be the director of a college. The director wore a white cloth wrapped around his waist. He raked his naked chest with his fingernails, partially smothered his yawns, and offered us the guest house for the night.

Reluctantly, the wet darkness revealed a complex stone shape. A weak lamp was burning on the veranda surrounded by watchful columns. We walked past the heavy ornamental fence, down the flooded path squeezed by the overgrown branches and filled with the fragrance of flowers, and up the streams running in torrents down the steps.

There, at the top, we saw the door. The doors on our planet only seem to be made of wood; they only seem to be indifferent. Actually, they are overly fragile, red-hot, potentially explosive. It is not only dangerous to touch them, it is best not to look at them at all.

The floorboards inside creaked, a lamp was lit, the lock clanked. The light tried to carry a woman into infinity, but she got stuck in the crack of the insufficiently opened door. She stood there, surrounded by the electric dust fluttering nervously around her, fixing her sleep-tousled hair, and wrapped in a skimpy robe, buttoned up hastily and not entirely.

In tired and nervous voice I explained to two green eyes that we were given permission to spend the night in the house. The woman said something in Hindi to the driver and he obediently nodded and disappeared into the downpour. Shaking off the monsoon like a dog, I carried its weakening reminders after her beautifully sculpted legs. We entered a dimly lit hall with heavy furniture from the beginning of the century. Bare and smooth ceiling beams resembled long bare legs. With my tongue still shaking from the vibrations of the road, I announced my name.

"Miss Kay," she answered absentmindedly.

"Where are you from?"

"What?" she yawned in her fist. "I am from America. From Iowa."

Iowa. I remembered my bleeding gums hurt by biting the hard and fuzzy honey-sweet quince, called in

Russian *ayva*. Iowa. A name like that would fit a woman from another planet.

"And I am from Russia," I said.

"Oh, really!" She transformed her *Oh* into the emptiness of a yawn.

"Your room is there," she pointed to one of the doors leading from the hall, and walked past me on her delicate legs towards a dresser worthy of a museum.

I imagined a pink glow bathing the setters lying near the fireplace, the ringing of an old grandfather's clock, *Romeo and Juliet* with its spine up, a silvery sound of a bell, and a maid running into the room. The hostess gives her instructions, "The guests are staying for the night; go, prepare fresh sheets for them. . . ."

"Excuse me," said Miss Kay, hanging on her wrist, one after another, pieces of ironed sheets for my tired body, "but there are no mosquito nets here. Don't be afraid, the night will be cool, and the cool air scares the mosquitoes away."

What cool air is she talking about? I protested in Russian, not aloud and somewhat to the side, like in a play by Chekhov. The air had been replaced by water, warmed up by someone in heaven. But even if the night happened to be cool. . . .

"Are you hungry?" Miss Kay interrupted my thoughts, in which I was warming her up right there, on those white sheets.

She put the entire refrigerator at my disposal. I selected cold chicken, fruit, and a bottle of whisky. Miss Kay wanted to leave right away, but I convinced her to stay. She reluctantly sat under the lamp and immersed herself in a thick volume. Bored by silence, I turned an old radio on. After some beeps, noise, and din, the receiver filled my soul with a familiar song: *Yesterday, love was such an easy game to play.* . . . I found myself in the twilight, on Blok's little iron bridge across the stream. Its turbulent current kept hitting the rocks, hurling the splashes to my feet and turning them into intricate spots with unclear but important meaning.

"Much obliged," I thanked her for the supper, pleasantly weakened by whisky and hors d'oeuvres and ready for intimate conversation. For conversation, which would lead to knowing each other better, to growing trust, to a spark of feeling, perhaps even to fireworks.

"Pleasant dreams," she wished and substituted her departing legs for everything that could have happened.

I'd like to be honest with you, Miss Kay. I'd like to be open. I had just enough to drink. You are standard, like a new bestseller, like a McDonald's, like a barbecue with a chat about kids and weather. I don't know why you need India, but you live here, like in Iowa—predictably, not romantically. I submit that our entire life is a tiring road, with women and men resembling little towns on the way. We stop in them for one night, for several days, for a month, even till death—and yet we don't stop there for eternity. So why shouldn't we use this eternally non-eternal moment to the fullest? Why should we, in a given situation, behave in a boring and banal way? Isn't this an extraordinary plot: India, the night, tropical downpour, a bungalow of an English colonist, fate throws two people into it, both of them are young, handsome, educated, smart, from great and very different countries— tell me what else is needed to become really interested in each other?

Her white legs were leaving, killing a good plot. They did not understand my ideas. Maybe I shouldn't have thought in Russian, I should have thought in English. But even though I was disappointed, my eyes did not leave her legs, but, like a true gentleman, followed them while their whiteness was still visible; and even after the legs vanished, my eyes accompanied them, in imagination, up to her bed, under her sheets. Under the sheets I lost my breath, comforted my throat with a glass of whisky, and went to my room.

Squinting at a low-hanging and bare light-bulb, I looked at about ten motionless lizards on the ceiling, frozen like ten unfulfilled hopes. I cringed, seeing how large moths and a hungry flock of mosquitoes were dying to get from the outside through the window screen; they sensed the emptiness in my disappointed soul and tried to fill it.

It's not her fault that we misunderstood each other. It was my fault that, as many times before, I did not have the courage to express my feelings to a woman honestly and directly, and in a sadly familiar way these feelings froze, just like those slippery-cold lizards. At night, one after another, they'll keep getting unglued from the ceiling, they'll keep falling on my bed, and they'll keep running over my body with their tiny and prickly feet.

And that's all for today. Now it's time to pretend that this new bed is more precious than everything else in the world. In my imagination, I dressed the bed in white, while in reality, on the contrary, I undressed completely. I turned off the light and lay on the bed like on an un-loved bride. In the carnival revelry of the downpour I recognized with disgust one insignificantly tiny sound. Buzzing. Today I won't be able to fall asleep. Without a mosquito net this one sound will turn into a biting million. I kept looking into an invisible corner at an invisible mosquito. . . .

Early at dawn I'll be awakened by singing of birds and by the sound of gardeners' hoes. I'll remember that I am a colonist, and with a cigar in my teeth I'll walk out to my garden. The flowers will wipe their wet faces with my spacious nightgown from Bukhara. The head servant will offer me a glass of juice and bend his head questioningly. "Horse!" I'll give him an order, jump in the saddle, and with a mighty squeeze of my calves force the horse from the spot into a gallop. The fresh morning will hit my face and the horse will carry me to the top of a hill. I'll see squares of water as far as the horizon. Over the surface of the squares, rippling the pale sky, slowly wades a flock of cranes taught to line up—bony people on skinny legs. Under their bloated stomachs, my rice ripens silently, but surely. It is harvested twice a year and it transforms miraculously: it acquires the most delicate colors of the dawn, it develops the ability to look as if it shone through the early dewy fog. In other words, having exchanged the rice for pearls, I am sending it to Europe and there, for a good reward, I strew it about female necks, drop it, but not completely, from naked tiny ears, carefully place it, lest it may roll off, on their genuinely weak fingers.

What is Miss Kay doing now? Is she sleeping, reading a book, thinking about something? Or, having found herself in Bombay and having mounted a cork board, she kicks her maddening legs in the ocean waters of the swimming pool and in the hearts of all the officers who hand her from the shore fruit cocktails and little notes. She looks at the notes and throws them away. Rocking in the tiny waves stirred by her kicking legs, the carelessly rejected admirers absorb water, become heavier, and land on the bottoms of glasses filled with strong British drinks. What a pity the girl from Iowa is not a daughter of an English colonist.

Through the walls I saw her white legs sticking out from under the sliding sheet cover. Trying not to bump into the things, driven insane from their longevity, I crossed the dimly lit hall, got to the corridor, and stopped. The light bulb was shining from the veranda through the glass. It was shining to allow the shadows of water drops to roll in blurs down the grey walls, and to make scorched shadows of the moths toss about and pulse. I stole up to her door. I was successfully preserving the silence, but it was treacherously broken by one darned floorboard.

"Go to sleep," the door advised.

Oh, how many hours of my life did I spend with beating heart next to their doors, only to hear this advice. Sometimes I dejectedly assumed I heard it more often than other men did, but I knew how to cheer myself up by a comforting thought that, apparently, I took more chances with women than other men did. But I have to explain; I kept hanging around the doors not only because of women's sweet bodies. A crazy and strange pitiless force often drowned me in the tender and melting depths of women's beautiful eyes, as if the meaning of life could be found there.

"Miss Kay, I see that you also cannot sleep. So what? Why should our insomnia torment us? I could sit on your bed, on its very edge. . . . We could have a great conversation."

The door was silent for a long time.

"Alright. Wait for me in the hall."

The hall was much better than nothing. The hall hid in itself possible continuations. Half-prone and squinting my eyes, I made myself comfortable on a sofa and left only one place for her to sit, a place between my chest and my knees. The pale circle of the radio's tuner, the only and sufficient illumination, extracted from the hall only the closest things: an armchair, a coffee table, and some journals. Music for intimacy. . . .

The squint of my eyes was sharply widened by the scissors-legs sticking out from under the robe. The lowest button was undone. Absentmindedness or design? She ceremoniously sat on the edge, not next to me on the sofa, on the prepared spot, but two cold steps away from me, on the old stiff leather of the armchair. She yawned into her fist. She looked down, at her sparkling knees. She felt too embarrassed to button her robe and placed her palms on her knees. Her eyes reflected the scale of the tuner and in the scale the entire planet was fighting sleep.

"Have you been here long?" I asked with feeling.

"A year. A little bit more."

"Aren't you missing Iowa yet?"

"No, not yet."

"And I miss Russia."

She yawned again. And did not say anything.

"And to be honest," I said dishonestly, "I don't miss it at all. India is beautiful and endless. Like a girl that you love."

She scratched in her armpit.

"You teach something in the college?" I tormented out questions.

She yawned, "Eh? Art history."

I tried to come up with a question about some art. There are many kinds of art in the world. What art precisely should I ask about? Well, there is, for instance, the art of love. Or the art of making friends. Or counterfeit money. Or real. . . . And then, what is art? I got alarmed, panicked, and lost the momentum and inertia. She used my hesitation to stretch out, get up from the armchair and say in a tired voice:

"Excuse me. It's too late. I have to get to the college in the morning."

Ah, how very similar you all are. Like easily-frightened cats, seemingly homeless, you cross the path of good men yearning for companionship. A man will walk up just to pet you, but you'll lower yourself on your half-bent paws, glance rapaciously and distrustfully, and disappear at full speed under the gate.

"Wait a moment," I said.

She remained half-turned.

"You're probably married," I guessed.

"Why?"

Because. . . . I fell in love with you. I don't know how deeply; I don't know if I fell in love for long, but at this moment I have a feeling that I fell in love with you devil-only-knows-how. And you are probably not married. All right, let's assume that you are married. Let's say that I am not alone either.

"I doubt if I'll be able to fall asleep," I answered.

"And I am dying to go to sleep," she said after yawning honestly.

I accompanied her to the hall. She turned towards the slightly opened and creaking entrance door, and stretched her hand towards the latch. Extending my hand faster than Miss Kay, I pushed the double door with evil force. The halves swung open willingly and we found ourselves in front of the downpour. I put my unruly hand on the edge of her thin shoulder, and with my other hand drove down her smooth nape, like down the children's slide. She became tense. For a long time we did not live, but stood, like an unfinished sculpture, in front of the pouring rain.

With an interrupted sigh, she turned around and offered me her weak lips. I've already congratulated myself on a victory, when suddenly she abruptly detached herself.

"Oh no. No! Please. No!"

Fine. I dropped my hands. Without looking back, she ran to her room. I turned towards the streams from the roof. In vain the heavens tried to exaggerate my endurable chagrin into violent sobs of suffering. Should we wipe off the spit and calmly hide under the ceiling with immobile lizards? Or should we cleverly explain to ourselves that this was not a defeat, but an ambiguous movement of fate? Or should we stubbornly refuse to accept it? Unsure what was better, I went to look for advice from the whisky bottle.

The door hook in Miss Kay's room clicked; she locked herself from the inside. Well, that's really too much! I gulped a good portion and stepped with the bottle under the warm flood.

Wait a moment. . . . I've been always gentle with women, I explained to everything in the world, slightly scared by making my way through poisonous swarms in seething deep puddles (maybe I made up the scorpions, vipers, poisonous toads and tarantulas, but if you don't make up anything, life turns into a grey wall that you follow everyday on the way to your stupefying work). As soon as I understood that one should not particularly trust women's words and actions, I began to refine my attempts to make them relaxed, get them to trust me, guess the meaning of their glances, gestures, words, and even of their silences. Of course, I was often mistaken, but mistakes of those who take risks can be corrected by other attempts. On the contrary, those who don't take risks make a mistake that cannot be corrected. Not abandoning my hopes for success, I used to agree to any kind of compromise and admired with gratitude everything that I encountered on my way, and everything that I encountered I turned into pleasant and beautiful storms in a glass—into peculiar little erotic storms revealed in the form of a naked knee, a squeal, fleeting expressions on the face, a laugh-wrinkle between eyebrows, changes of lines in the region of the neck, breast or waist. . . .

Sleep, Miss Kay, I continued aloud. Sleep with dignity, virtuously. In proud unblemished loneliness. Hoping that your future husband, an American with a dependable job, will appreciate your innocence. He'll help you fulfill all of your female worldly dreams: a house of your own, a couple of kids, evenings with cocktails by the fireplace, trips to Florida and Hawaii, Saturday dinners in restaurants, a few friendly families who can pleasantly talk about Academy Awards, diet and weight loss, childbearing according to Spock, cars and insurance. In the morning I won't see you anymore. You will go to teach art, or art history, and I will lie around as long as I want, then take a shower, have a relaxed breakfast, get into my car, and ask my driver to take me to the next little town. Since I know that in the upcoming towns everything will be basically the same, I am prepared for the same, but I am not losing hopes for an interesting innovation. In any case, you cannot argue with the old German saying: *New town—new girls.*

But maybe I have made a mountain out of a molehill? Maybe you also don't have anything against all that, but you have PMS? Or, perhaps you are frigid? Or a lesbian? Maybe you have a venereal disease? Excuse me, of course. I am drunk and depressed. I understand that these thoughts, in grandiloquent terms, do not befit a true gentleman. Frankly speaking, what is left for the undeservedly rejected men? They are left with suppositions similar to mine. But unlike the majority, I am a just man. If one could scoop out with a bucket the dirt from the bottom of the well of my failure, do you know who will happen to be at the bottom? I. Not you, Miss Kay, but only I—the initial cause of my fiasco. But not of a depressing one. Of a colorful, bitterly-sweet fiasco. Because bitterness can be easily sweetened by the increasingly keen interest in that what will come after you. You cannot even imagine how much was left for me besides your snowy-white, undeniably sweet body. In addition to the thoughts described above and to particular feelings associated with them, other women were left for me, and, according to the theory of probability, sooner or later some of them wouldn't reject me. And, most importantly, the daughter of the English colonist (in other words, my imagination) was also left intact.

Today, she is probably an old woman. She lives in a spacious house in Manchester. In the basement there is a trunk, filled to the brim with pearls from India. She hates to sell them and she is too lazy to do it. A head of a tiger with a broken lower jaw stands on the trunk. The tiger is a memory of her father, who has shot it himself, although the stuffing has been done by someone else.

During the rainy days the woman sits by the window. The raindrops stream down the windowpanes. They are running, stopping, swelling, merging, crawling away. Unpredictable. Impulsive. Reckless. Romantic. Like people whose lives are not boring.

An unexpected afterword

After finishing work on this story, I decided to show the manuscript to a friendly family that lived nearby in the wilderness of the snowy mountains not far from the Canadian border.

The March snow was having a fit. The wind howled. The telephone, almost dead, came alive.

"This is me," said Alyona, a member of the mentioned family, "an easily-frightened and seemingly homeless cat. That's what you call women, right?"

"Look how Vladimir suffered," I said, defending the hero's behavior, "while Miss Kay only kept yawning. What a lack of sensitivity, indeed. . . ."

"It seems that you don't know women very well. . . ."

In short, an exchange of gunfire followed and the ancient misunderstanding between women and men was not only preserved, but even increased in intensity.

I thought that this was the end of our discussion of the story. I was wrong. Two weeks later, Alyona sent me her own manuscript, that is, her retelling of the story in Miss Kay's words. My reaction? I was surprised and felt awkward. But not too much.

Anyway, here it is, Miss Kay's story written by Russian Alyona.

THE BLUE-EYED STONES

As you know, it is easier to fall asleep when it rains. But today, the noise of tropical monsoon was bringing in memories, not sleep. I must have been missing my home; in my fantasies the monsoon turned into a rainstorm in Iowa, while I was just a girl with two red pony tails. Our creaking, mooing, and cackling farm seemed to quiet down under the rain, and it filled up with ripe smells of wet soil, leaves, grass, and damp old wood.

During the rains I often got sad and found myself in front of a figurine of an unknown Eastern god, placed by my parents among condiments and spices. I would take the idol down from the shelf and look carefully at his effeminate face with its mysterious smile and squinting glance. Glistening with matte bronze, he danced in a circle of fire, raising his rounded feminine leg and trampling some devil with the other. His four hands were weaving to the music. I imagined that he danced for me. It seemed as if he had picked me out of all others and with his mysterious dance tried to tell me something important.

Much later, I completely baffled my practical farmer-parents by becoming a student of art history and taking my bronze dancer to New York. I soon learned a lot about him. His name was Shiva, and in far-away India he was considered a god of destruction. He was an angry, but, at the same time, compassionate god; he kept destroying to create anew. And when college ended with an offer to go to the distant and mysterious Ahmednagar, I knew: this was the will of my Shiva, tired of the noisy bustle of New York. And it's been a year since I moved into the spacious empty guest house and began teaching dark-headed bronze-skinned students art history.

Despite the noise of the rain and all these thoughts I was able to fall asleep, but the sleep was ended by a knock on the door. On such a night and at such an hour? Wrapping myself in my robe, I hurried to the entrance door. In the violent warm streams from heaven, a dim light-bulb found a tall stranger. He had blonde hair, a soft gaze, and an open, tired smile.

"I was given permission to spend the night here," the stranger began to explain with an accent.

Still half-asleep, I looked at large drops falling from his eyelashes on his cheeks and running down his strong neck under his collar.

"Yes, yes, of course. Come in, please."

"My name is Vladimir," he introduced himself.

"Miss Kay," I answered.

I led him in, showed him the room, took fresh sheets from the dresser. I felt his attentive look. Warm, manly, and strangely exciting. I felt that I blushed, so I turned abruptly and asked:

"You're probably hungry?"

My mother told me that women feel pleasure when they feed men. I looked at the eating stranger and I agreed with mother completely. He kept asking me about the college, India, and Iowa. He poured himself some whisky and drank it in one gulp. Avoiding his eyes, I looked at his hands, large, nervous, and handsome. Then, I looked into his face, but when I found a tender azure, I immediately turned away, embarrassed.

"Pleasant dreams!" I started walking, without looking back, feeling his eyes on my legs.

I was lying in my room, defended by the coverlet pulled up to my chin. How blue his eyes are! Like the tiny veins on mother's hands, like the thin ballerinas of Degas, like the roads in Iowa, like the nights here, in India. Who is he? He said he was from Russia. Snow, Tchaikovsky, Anna Karenina, Dostoevsky, nesting dolls, chicken Kiev—this list almost exhausted my entire knowledge of Russia. Plus—Chagall's pictures, with a couple in love flying over a sleepy town. What if this Vladimir is an artist? And what will happen if he stays here for a long time? In the mornings he'll be leaving with his easel in the direction of the sun rising above rice fields, and in the evenings he'll be returning excited and tired. I will be frying rice and *chappati* for him—the way I have been taught in India. And then we will go to Russia together. Vladimir will show me the places where he grew up, and introduce me to his mother. We will go to a concert of Tchaikovsky. During the concert, he will whisper that he loves me more than music and painting. And then he'll take me to a church. With high arches, with a smell of wax, with flames of the candles—just like in the movies. I will wear a white bridal dress and hold a heavy bouquet of white roses. The church choir will sing for us. Russian saints will smile on us from the icons. . . .

Ah, why are you teasing me, Shiva? Why are you trying to convince me that you brought me to India for a purpose, and that this night, this torrential rain, and Vladimir—that all this is not accidental?. . . How funny! I am thinking about him so much and he probably has been asleep for a long time. . . .

I heard the sound of careful steps on a creaking floor. My heart started beating madly.

"Go to sleep," I heard my own voice.

It is quiet. He's still there. Is it possible that my silly fantasies are coming true?. . .

"Miss Kay, I see that you also cannot sleep. . . ."

He was saying something else, but I did not understand him well. Don't answer, don't answer.

"All right," I heard my own voice. "Wait for me in the hall."

The main thing is to be distantly polite. And even better—boringly-sleepy, which is credible at such an hour. I turned helplessly towards the silhouette of my Shiva; then, I put on my robe and walked out of the room.

Vladimir was waiting, lying on the couch. I sat down in the armchair across from him, and I transformed a nervous deep sigh into a false yawn. But why did he lie down, instead of sitting up? If he was simply sitting, I would probably ask him about Russia and about Chagall. I would find out who he was and why he was here. He kept asking trivial questions and I answered in monosyllables. I cursed myself that I came out, but some strange force was drawing me to sit next to him, to bend over him. And—to kiss his azure eyes, touch his light hair, dip my face in his hands. No, this was intolerable. I got up from the armchair.

"I have to be at the college in the morning."

He followed me closely, like a warm wave. I reached towards the latch to lock the entrance door. Before I could do it, Vladimir pushed the door open. His hand burned my nape with tenderness. The world stumbled and started floating. I turned around and pressed myself to his lips. I was becoming weaker in his passionate embrace; I trembled, couldn't catch my breath. Suddenly I felt his greedy fingers. And I saw his face, distorted by impatience.

"Oh no. Please, no!"

I was running away from him the same way I was running once in my childhood, after I looked into a deep dried-up well. I swung into it with such horror, as if some dark depth tried to pull me to the bottom.

I threw myself on the bed and buried my face in the pillow, swallowing tears. It seemed to me that I heard my Shiva laugh at me. He was making faces, scaring me with his evil squint, trampling me with his bronze legs and burning me with his circle of fire. Why did you choose me when I was a child? Why did you bring me to this India? Why did you throw me in the azure of his eyes, and then so mercilessly poked fun at me? Why did you, Shiva, destroy everything again? What do you want to create instead? Do you want me to find quickly a reliable husband, have children, become a housewife, and then find a job close to my house? Just so I can sigh tiredly in the evening: well, again, another day has passed by, another month, another year? . . .

I was trembling, like the rain on the other side of the window. And I felt that I slowly dissolved in the tropical downpour, turned into narrow streams and, hurt and desperate, threw myself onto the sharp, slippery stones.

The White-eyed Saleswoman

If she had been lame as well, or humpbacked,
I might very likely have loved her even more. . . .

F. M. Dostoevsky. Crime and Punishment

1

The leaves of the lilac bush were moving peacefully between Alexandra's eyes and the blue expanse of the universe. Autumn is coming. Soon, all the leaves will get old, but they will stubbornly cling to the bush. Then, a bird will land on a branch, a cat will chase the bird, a cloud will shower the bush with cold raindrops, an insect will step on a leaf, the wind will blow or, with no outside intrusion, the leaves, unable to bear their own weight, will humbly detach themselves from life. Where will they go? Unsure, they will fill the air with this question, and their yellow corpses will whirl around. The sadist Pushkin will rejoice: *Oh mournful season that delights the eyes.* . . . During a damp night, the corpses of the leaves will turn into bats, and their wet touch on my face will frighten me. The clouds will break apart and crawl away. The leaves will freeze in the sky and start to shine. They will become falling stars. After piercing holes in the cold clouds, they will cheerlessly draw lines in heavens. Sleepily swaying in the saddle, I will look at snowy leaves landing on the horse's mane. . . .

"There's no vodka," Alexandra said, without looking at the person who touched her shoulder.

"I don't want vodka," the voice was Polina's. "We don't have enough black bread."

Alexandra did not answer. Lingering among the leaves that kept moving quietly on the other side of the window, she sat on the bed naturally, with her legs apart, her hands down, and her spine bent.

"So you won't come to see us either?"

"Us?" An echo jumped back at Polina.

"Alexandra, you know very well that the entire village is coming to my party. Do as you wish, I will not drag you there. But if you decide to come, bring some bread from the store."

Polina took a step across the threshold, but stopped in the open door, and turned around with a smile:

"You got dressed up, so why should I be different? Today I will put on such an outfit that all my guests will swoon. Would you want to know where I got it? Donat Vasilievich gave it to me!"

Eh, Polina, eh stupid woman, you'd better keep quiet about it! If you're going, be going where you need to go. Yet no, she'd stop, turn around, and flail her forked tongue.

"Wait a minute," said Alexandra with a big vacant smile, but sitting as she was before, not planning to take her marble-white eyes off the leaves. "Why did he give you a dress?"

"Why?" Polina smiled mysteriously. "As a gift for something."

Polina liked to play the slut. She constantly hinted to everybody about her easy victories over men. Of course, nobody believed in her victories; the village laughed at her, but without malice. The village was grateful to her for guaranteed entertainment in its monotonous existence, drenched by rains. People did not love her, but they understood that she was trying to avenge her unsuccessful external appearance. Village life in Russia, like an endless punishment with a knout, balances universal hostility with vague, but concrete compassion.

"A gift for what?" Alexandra asked absentmindedly.

She heard something in response, but could not make out what she heard; she was still preoccupied with the quiet green rustling between her eyes and the world.

2

Actually, instead of leaves, she saw there people with exactly the same faces, but different fates. These green people helped Alexandra remember her special day. On that day, a new teacher, a resident of the capital, came to the store for the first time. He came in and loudly said, "Good morning." While she was pouring buckwheat into a small bag and watching the scale's arrow, she seemed not to have heard his greeting.

Seeing Alexandra for the first time, one would certainly think: "Here's a typical saleswoman from a typical Russian god-forsaken place." She was gaunt, lanky, and unattractive, and her eyes seemed to be covered with white film. But her ability to perceive people by the way they spoke sharply increased since the time when she cried her eyes out. He came in and simply said, "Good morning," but in those two common words she heard good upbringing, intelligence, decency, dignity, tenderness, wisdom, and spiritual depth.

She was unable to resist the avalanche triggered by the two words spoken by the man who, as she already knew from hearsay, finished the Moscow University, worked abroad, knew foreign languages, was *terribly smart*, *tall*, and *handsome*, and who would live in the same little house, in which three graduates of the regional pedagogical institute, assigned and dispatched to work in the village, had lived for two months until they ran away. They were dispatched and ran away, but he came voluntarily. Everyone was wondering why, everyone tried to guess, and everyone kept making up various rumors, even implying that he was deported from Moscow for parasitism or politics.

She almost physically felt that after no more than two words the English teacher grew up to the ceiling and filled the room to the walls. Cramped, suffocating, and horrified, she dropped the packet of buckwheat and ran away through the back door. She stood there for a long time, hugging the sacks and listening to her heart, which sounded as hollow as if in her chest a frightened strong horse were galloping down a long wood-paved street.

3

Before the moment when we encountered Alexandra for the first time (on the bed, with her eyes turned to the leaves), fate succeeded in dividing her life into three different lives.

In the first life there were her mama and papa, the caretakers who loved her importunately. There were petty squabbles about every C, heart palpitations caused by every D and each five-minute tardiness, wobbly walks around St. Petersburg with her or with each other, always hand in hand; in the first life—Mama and Papa, like the milk, which boils over, constantly and hopelessly spilling on the stove top.

One day, the day of hope (between the final exams in high school and entrance exams to the institute), Papa and Mama, shuffling home from the bakery, were crossing the street and did not notice, or perhaps noticed too late, the huge Intourist bus stuffed with grey-haired foreigners.

Alexandra's new life crawled out from under the wheels of the grey-haired foreigners. Those, who gave her the first life, did not step discretely aside, as she had hoped before entering the institute, but on the contrary, filled her life even more with their maimed bodies. They overfilled it to such a degree that Alexandra, glancing with fear at an icon, wished that her parents had not given her the first life at all. In the beginning of this half-dead life both parents spent several months in various hospitals with traumas to intestines, spines, heads, and all other conceivable organs, extremities, and systems. Then, with no chance to ever get up and ever get better, they continued to lie in bed at home.

Instead of becoming a historian, she became a nanny to her mama and papa. To make money, she learned how to sew and type. Working on an order at her typewriter or sewing machine, she constantly felt on her back guilty and sad eyes her parents. They understood that they maimed their daughter's life, and they often cried because of that. And she cried about it more than her papa and mama together. Good God! Much more! She cried without stopping and salted everything with her tears.

She cried in the kitchen over a skillet. The tears jumped off it with a hiss and splattered the oil or sunk into potatoes, the family's basic food. She cried, kneeling and blindly rubbing the floor with a rag. She cried, bending over a toilet, emptying a bedpan into a bubbling stream. She cried over the typewriter and the sewing machine, and her tears broke into pieces on the black keys with white letters, as if those tears were pleading with the alphabet, with the rich Russian language, or they got absorbed by the things destined to be worn by others. She cried after occasional movies, and the passers-by turned around and away thinking that boys tricked and abandoned this girl, cheated by beauty. They did not know that the girl cried because no one ever tricked or abandoned her, never even kissed her on the cheek, never even looked so that she could get offended and shyly lower her eyes. She cried late in the evening, reading a page about love, and after that the page would wrinkle, becoming a wrinkled life among other, normal lives. She cried often in front of the mirror; she hated the mirror, but she tortured herself on purpose, studying her freckled face, which looked as if it were splattered with rust, with a long, sinuous nose curved to the side, with a thin protruding chin, with short and choppy red eyebrows, and with pale grey eyes framed by yellowish eyelashes as rough as a wire brush.

When she turned thirty-four, her papa and mama died on the same day. Papa went first, as he was, half-sitting on the pillows inserted by his daughter. Mama looked askance at Papa, saw him sitting there with an open mouth, with his head dropping unnaturally to the side, and blindly looking past her, so she dropped her head in Papa's direction and began looking past him.

After their death, Alexandra cried every day for two months. Then suddenly her tears had run out. Walking around the house with a dry face, she found herself in front of the mirror, looked in, habitually, for no reason at all, but instead of herself, she saw there a woman with marble-white eyes in a disappearing face.

She got frightened, jumped back, circled her small room for a long time and approached the mirror from the side. Then, horrified, as if she were looking into the open jaws of a beast, she stretched her neck, and, completely contorted, inserted her head into the reflection.

From the deep rectangle, as if from a hole in a white wall leading into a frightening unknown world, a vague female face stared at her with marble eyes. Alexandra forced herself to keep looking, but no matter how much she looked or turned, no matter from what angle she looked, she could not clearly see the woman's features.

She decided that all this was due to nerves, that after some time, perhaps as soon as the next morning, everything would become clear again. As for now, why should she be upset? Now, on the contrary, she should be merry. It does not matter what the others will see; from now on, at least for a while, she will not see her hated face in any mirror. For a while she will see in mirrors only what she wants to see. For instance, she will see beautiful women.

She smiled, went away from the mirror, and, humming a song, sat down at her sewing machine. For some pretty girl, she was making a maxi saturated by tears. The skirt's pattern spiraled in a whirlwind of bright, contrasting flowers, flying around the waist and down, around the hips and down, around the legs and down, and finally dropping to the floor. She was sewing with a dry happy face, as if she were making this beautiful skirt for herself. Hungry, she went to the kitchen, fried a lot of potatoes with onions, ate it all, went to bed, and slept like a log.

She woke up in the morning with a feeling of unusual anxiety. She thought that she had had a strange dream. She stayed in bed for a long time, thinking about the woman with white eyes. She got up, went to the bathroom, and on her way back to bed she saw in the mirror two white eyes on a face that kept slipping away.

The face pretended to be a beauty, but the beauty still had the same marble-white eyes. It was, rather, a bust of a beauty, a corpse with eyes pecked out, a specter, a vampire, a zombie, or an imp. She crossed herself three times, knocked on wood three times with her knuckle, and spat three times across her left shoulder.

Yesterday's thought that she had gone mad required some proof, but how could she go to a psychiatrist with that? The psychiatrist would listen to her story, look intently into her eyes, bend over the writing table and write for a long, long time. In the end, the story of the reflection would turn into a lifelong story of mental illness that the doctor would classify as paranoia with complications. He would brilliantly support his completely false diagnosis describing the shock caused by the bus accident, her endlessly-sick parents and, in general, her wasted life.

Beginning with this daybreak, she did not leave the mirror for God only knows how long—an hour, a day, perhaps even a year—nobody would ever know how long because she stood in front of the mirror without any witnesses at all. She stood there exactly as much time as was needed to come up with the usable, non-psychiatric answer to the riddle of her eyes.

She formulated this answer as follows: Drop after drop, her tears erased, washed out, dissolved the particles of pigment in her corneas until they turned white.

Was Alexandra's answer right? The readers' answer to this question will depend on whether they question everything or only certain things.

4

She got ready and left the house. Many people were on the street, but nobody looked at her because nobody ever looks at bony, stooping women in sack-like dark blue clothes, who walk like men, and hold old shopping bags in their hands. Alexandra's bag did swing strongly, as if it were hanging on a hook nailed to a shaft of a cart pulled by a horse.

Since her eyes were turned down or to the side, to the swinging shop windows, she did not look at the people. They passed her, fell behind or crossed her path, yet they were no more than quick, moderate, and slow-moving legs in pants, skirts, boots, and shoes. She raised her eyes slightly only at the moment when her turn came and she began her prepared phrase, "A hundred grams of butter, a can of green peas, a quarter kilo of farmer's cheese, and a loaf of bread."

She expected to see a face, which she always met there, the face of the saleswoman she knew, but instead she saw something vanishing, with incomprehensible features framed by curly hair. She got confused and, instead of the entire phrase, she was only able to say "A hundred gra. . . ." That *hundred gra* pierced the ears under the curls, like an incredible insult.

"Why'd ya come if ya don't know what ya want in the store?" asked the saleswoman in the language of petty dictators and the Russian mob, flourishing on shortages. Then she turned away from Alexandra and gawked at the next buyer with blazing eyes.

After she sliced some *Russian* cheese for him and turned her face to the queue, she again noticed Alexandra who, apparently, was mocking her by hanging around the counter.

"Look, people, she's still standing there! Why doesn't she leave? What did I tell ya? I won't be selling nothing if some psycho disrupts my work."

The queue responded with a hollow mutter. Now the shoppers hated Alexandra and loved the dictator.

The perpetual Russian shortages have created the dictatorship of saleswomen, who rule the people any way they want. The people mumble, but obey—exactly like a dog that licks any hand holding a piece of sausage. The people who obey the crude half-literate women do not need freedom or democracy, but a capricious strong dictator who will feed them first and then can even whip them. In gratitude, those well-fed and whipped people will lick the dictator's hand—and ass—if they are told to do so. This is not a new thought, but it's always actual for Russia.

"Excuse me, citizens, have you gone mad?" a lively male voice was heard from the queue. "Don't you see that she is blind?"

Everybody noticed that the scandalous one was daringly white-eyed.

"Why didn't you say so right away? A hundred grams of what? Speak!"

Again, Alexandra did not answer. She moved her white eyes, punctured in the center, from face to face, and could not distinguish anyone, perhaps only women from men. The entire store queue consisted of twins with indescribable grey faces.

"And she's deaf too! Who lets them out on the street?"

Turning away from Alexandra, who was standing there as if she were petrified, the saleswoman implied she had more important things to do than to move this dead tree. The other customers quickly lowered their eyes, afraid to attract the attention of the white-eyed, deaf, and probably insane woman.

Somehow she recovered and slowly dragged herself home. All the people she met on the way resembled each other like water drops. She looked at one drop, then at another, and she saw each disappear, as if the earth absorbed them, as if her glances burned them and turned them to vapor. And again, passers-by did not look at her, or, noticing her silhouette, they got annoyed or upset, thinking that she was obstructing what they could otherwise see.

Not immediately, but after she got used to the new image of the human race, Alexandra lowered her eyes again, and the human race turned again into hems, stockings, cuffs, and socks. Now, whispers, hisses, hushed laughter, surprised cries, silence, broken conversations, heavy sighs, or garbled words haunted her everywhere.

She decided to leave the city. But where should she go? She did not know where. It would have been great to seek someone's advice, but how could she impose on strangers a question of this kind: "Couldn't you advise me what would be the best place for me to go?" She had a vague feeling that she should go to a village. Well, fine. But which village?

She saw a recurring dream: She would be riding a horse, someone would be embracing her from behind, the horse would quietly walk down a narrow path, and she would sway in the saddle, pushing aside soft branches of birch trees. Perhaps it was just a fantasy, or she dreamed a dream from her great-grandmother's life, or it was a village she had visited as a small girl with her papa and mama? Or maybe this sunny dream vision was so bright and joyous not because of the atmosphere of the village, but because a man was embracing her while she was sitting on the horse?

Whatever the reason, Alexandra entrusted her third life to a completely accidental village.

5

A bored peasant rarely visits an establishment chosen by the authorities as a place intended to end village boredom. There are roughly two establishments like that in the village: a library and a club—that's all. But peasants don't like libraries. Paging through the journal *Ogonyok*, they get tense, confused, annoyed by the presence of the librarian, Lilka, whose eyes clearly convey the idea that she cannot comprehend what in the world, besides a shovel, a cow, and vodka, could interest a peasant. Movies at the club are rare and usually very old. Generally speaking, the club is a dark cave, in which teenagers squeal and cackle, and Vysotsky and foreign singers wheeze. The peasant jumps out on the street, scratches his nape, starts walking in no particular direction, and invariably finds himself in front of the only store in the village.

In the store, one can say hello to the saleswoman and to those who are already there; one can listen to the babble of a group of women, touch the fabric one doesn't need, ask about the next delivery of sugar, turn towards the squeaking door and scrutinize the customer who just entered, interrupt a woman spinning a tale about a flying cow ("You're full of shit!"), make eyes to a young woman buying two bottles of vodka ("Are you going to share?"), or energetically greet a robust peasant sitting gloomily on the window sill ("How are things, Grisha?").

The store is also a good place to let the tension out. If you have a compellingly important reason, you can run in there with a shotgun and blast away from both barrels. It is best to aim at a lamp because the ensuing panic in inadequate light is exactly what you need. If your reason is more moderate, you can get into a simple fight. Tiny reasons can be deflated by swearing into people's faces or behind their back.

Finally, the peasant comes to the poorly-stocked village store to satisfy his everyday needs, to find out that he cannot satisfy them or to ignore them with the help of vodka.

We should note the following specific characteristic of the store of our particular village. Before entering it, the peasants freed themselves of mud and snow with an almost clinical effort, using the puddles, pieces of wood and rocks, stomping their feet, knocking, and kicking; they brushed off the snow from their collars and hats, and then quietly, scrupulously, but as quickly as they could, dealt with the tough, reinforced door and greeted the saleswoman with an ingratiating, "Hello, Miss Alexandra."

Such courteous behavior of the peasants, not quite common for the country of boors, barbarians, and thieves, could be explained by the fact that nobody was able to predict how Alexandra would react to a particular visitor. She might ignore him completely. She might hug him and kiss him. Or she might laugh, curse, chuckle, spit furiously, start singing a merry song, or throw the package down and disappear in the supply room.

But the peasants forgave Alexandra everything. They forgave her, of course, because she was one of the dictators, but more so for her honesty, hard-work, and efficiency; that is, they forgave her twofold. They considered her slightly insane not on the basis of her capricious behavior, but because even when that living unpredictability stared at them point-blank, her frighteningly-white eyes were still unable to see.

She did not keep livestock at home and did not have a garden, since she worked in the store from seven in the morning till eight in the evening, and on weekends peasants occasionally came to her house and begged her to run to the store for vodka. She either bluntly refused or, on the contrary, ran right away to fetch it. But since sometimes she was, without concern for positions, understanding with the lads and strict with the chairman, no customers were offended by her behavior, and when they complained, they felt that they were complaining about their fate.

6

Polina often lied about her victories over village men, but she did not lie about getting the best dress in the village from Donat. After she knocked on Donat's door and a raspy voice inside answered, Polina contrived to look with interest at absolutely uninteresting things in the hall: felt boots, shoes, rusty bucket, and sacks with potatoes, cabbage, and onions. A short fur-coat, a padded jacket, a rusty saw blade, and a roll of string were hanging from rusty nails sticking out of the logs.

The hook clicked, the door was pulled back, and a man with uncombed hair appeared in the open space.

He was wearing a bright Eastern robe. On his naked chest, in the triangle of the collar, was a cross made of black wood. The bottom of the robe was folding around slippers with sharply-curved tips, resembling the ones worn by fairy-tale wizards.

Polina stepped back from the door. But this wasn't the city or a building with many floors, where you could think you made a mistake.

"Why are you afraid?" The robe sounded like a sleepy landowner of the last century.

"What makes you think that I am afraid?" Polina answered the question with a question, sailing inside.

Donat closed the heavy door, bent over the wash-bowl under the wash-stand, filled a cup made of his hands with water and said before he began splashing,

"You can sit down on the bed for now."

"Thank you." Polina sat on the edge of the bed.

Besides the bed, in the spacious room with a Russian stove there was a bench with two buckets and a water canister, a veneer wardrobe, a pile of luggage, and a curtain with leaves falling in the wind. It concealed a good quarter of the room. Polina looked at the falling leaves longer than at anything else. Yes, the curtain was really nice, but it was hiding something unknown; that wasn't fair.

Bent over the basin, with water dripping from his face, Donat glanced at Polina and smiled as if he knew the thoughts brought to her mind by the falling leaves. It seemed to him that the falling leaves induced in her some idea about a magnificent alcove, hiding a pair of semi-naked beauties, who, sprawling on the satin sheets, smoked foreign cigarettes, drank champagne from crystal glasses, and ate pineapple chunks.

He smiled and continued splashing. But he guessed wrong. Staring at the leaves chased by the strong autumn wind, Polina was imagining the legendary piece of Italian stretch-fabric in Donat's luggage.

She heard about it from her daughter who, with a few of her girlfriends, visited the teacher every day while his hand was healing. They bought him groceries, made his food, washed floors, and did the laundry. And he told them about India, Moscow, and many other things. Using a sheet as a screen, he showed them slides, allowed them to play with the tape recorder, and recited unknown poets from memory.

One day, he showed them a suitcase with various curious souvenirs. Among the souvenirs was a length of a strange fabric, which shimmered, like a gold fish. The piece could be put over one's head, almost like a stocking; it was astonishingly stretchy, and all the girls tried it on; it fit everyone, everyone looked great in it, and everyone loved it. "It would fit you easily, too," said Lariska, looking at her mother with an eye of a saleswoman or a tailor. "You'd only need to cut openings for hands and hem the edges so they wouldn't fray."

Polina remembered the fabric; she even dreamed about putting it on and bargaining about it with Donat.

7

The splashing and snorting ended. Polina turned her eyes away from the curtain, towards Donat, and he, so large and bright, drying his face with a towel, looked at her with a smile and asked:

"Well, did you like the falling leaves?"

Polina did not need to think about it. She was one of those people who always talk without thinking.

"They're nice, the colors are pretty. While you were washing, I kept looking and I thought it would be great to have a dress like that."

"The fabric is from India," said Donat. "They know how to work with fabric there."

"I wish I could see what kinds of fabric they have." Polina came closer to her secret goal.

"Well, you see it." Donat pointed to the curtain.

Disappointed, Polina cursed to herself. Did she come here to discuss the damned curtain? Well, never mind. She sighed.

"Yes, in India they know how to make things."

"Some things they know, and some they don't," said Donat as he gave the canister with water a few pats with his palm. "In India everything made of iron is expensive and of poor quality. They have a low level of mechanization."

"To hell with mechanization!" She breathed out this last word, indistinct and metallic, awfully-dreary and repulsive to all, with such passion, that Donat thought with remorse she was cursing her husband, a tractor operator and a mechanic.

"Don't swear!" said Donat. "Without that mechanization you'd still milk the cows by hand."

"You don't know, so better shut up!" she said angrily.

But she stopped herself immediately. She's come here to ask for something and now she's being rude. That's not right, she has to be kinder. When you deal with women you need to think from which angle you should approach them, but with men you'd do better in bed. This way, you'd get anything you wish. Aristocratic women asked post factum for diamonds, houses, carriages, whatever they wanted. And during the war, after sleeping with a German officer, one of our female scouts was able to find out the locations of enemy's tank divisions.

"Don't argue," she said tenderly. "Better come to our farm and see with your own eyes, what kind of mechanization we have. Sewage station, that's all."

"Sewage — you're right here. The smell is so strong that one could hang an axe in the air. No, I do not want to see it with my own eyes. My clothes will start smelling and I'll drown in the mud. . . ."

"So how come I don't smell?" Polina got angry, but immediately forced herself to calm down. "And, as you can see, I have not drowned in the mud yet."

Donat sat with his back against the logs. He hugged the sink and the bucket, closed his eyes and sat silently for a while. After yesterday's drinking he felt shaky and nauseous.

"It's my hangover," he explained. I drank alone yesterday. What a concert I gave of my own memories! Even in the Kremlin Palace of Congresses you wouldn't see a better one."

"The Palace of Congresses!" Polina sighed. "I'd like to take a look at it."

"Don't you know that in the Palace they give spectacles and concerts for the general public? It is a beautiful building, in which all those, who want to do so, can breathe the same air that the government breathes, can walk on carpets, up and down the halls and stairs, along which the government walks, go to the sparkling restrooms used by the government, or take an elevator to the floor just under the roof to a banquet hall, in which on every appropriate occasion the government toasts the health of the people. One can even sit in a gigantic auditorium, in which the government makes important decisions. In other words, my dear Polinochka, this is a building, in which, after you get there, you feel a gratifying, gentle excitement, as if by some miraculous chance you found yourself in the apartments of the tsars, stretched out on the luxurious tsarist bed, and expected the monarch to come in any second."

Polina opened her eyes widely. She sat for a while in a stupor. Finally she left the fairy tale and, coming back to normal life, narrowed her eyes ironically.

"They eat there like kings, and how about us? Come to the store and, like an idiot, you'll stand in front of that flounder with white film over her eyes. There's no meat, no fish, no dairy products, no fruit, not even vegetables. Only canned stuff and old crackers. If they bring frozen cod, there is a queue starting at the very door. But when you defrost this cod, it smells rotten, you better hold your nose. And why is there nothing to wear? I've already worn my only holiday dress to shreds. Yes, sometimes they bring stuff. So what? I don't see it. Why? Because everything is done illegally. And I am not used to kissing somebody's ass."

"You should be used to it," said Donat. "If you want to have things, know how to kiss ass."

"Whose ass? This white-eyed flounder's? That's going too far. Excuse me, please."

Donat did not answer. They were silent for a while. Polina coughed discreetly into her plump fist.

"Yes, the colors are quite nice. It would be great to have something like this for a dress. Otherwise now I feel completely naked."

Provoked by these words, Donat undressed her with his eyes. Polina caught his look and pulled her very faded dress with daisies over her plump knees.

"What are you saying? You are completely undressed and on the bed, while I am dressed and stand on the cold floor?" asked Donat.

Any woman would laugh if a man hinted to her about having sex, especially if he did the hinting standing on the cold floor in warm Indian slippers with sharply-curved tips.

"On the cold floor?" She started laughing. "And you're wearing slippers, like an old wizard."

From laughing hard, Polina fell on the bed, and her head landed straight on the pillow. The daisies sneaked up towards her stomach, and her underwear appeared shamelessly. Donat looked at the underwear and at the strip of her white belly. . . .

8

The merchant sat on the floor of his shop and observed through his half-closed-eyes the swarms of people in the narrow street. As soon as Donat, walking aimlessly, stopped in front of the shop and his eyes tried to penetrate its semi-darkness, the merchant jumped up, ran up to him, made an inviting sign with his hand, and mumbled in an acceptable English:

"Please, Saab, sit down, Saab. I have the best selection of fabrics, the best quality, dirt cheap."

After finishing the performance of the first part of the program, that is, after attracting the foreigner to his store, nailing him to soft pillows, closing his mouth with an icy-cold Coca-Cola, and turning on the fan, the merchant, not really interested in what exactly the saab needed, began to produce all of the store's merchandise with the speed and dexterity of a magician. The goal of the second part of the program was to astound, overwhelm the client, make him ashamed that because of him the store is being turned upside down.

A dark-skinned boy, as thin as a bean, kept handing the rolls of fabric to the owner, and the latter kept throwing them towards the opposite side of the store; the rolls, unfolding fast, drew a semicircle in the air, and each new semicircle floated to the ground as a part of the rainbow. The light-green fabric did not have time to land, and the light lilac one was already unfurling above it. The merchant held in his hands a roll of thin yellow pillow-lace, and, at the same moment, the boy was handing him a roll of pink nylon with large flowers.

When the merchant unrolled the falling leaves, Donat said, "I'll take that." He had never bought any fabric before and did not expect to say these words, but the merchant hoped to hear them from the moment the foreigner entered his store.

Donat was dragged into the store by the merchant, but he would have freed himself and gone away, if at that moment the salesman did not wave in front of his nose the frosty Coca-Cola. After exhausting heat, the bottle looked like a dream, and Donat gave up and sat on the prepared pillows.

"You mean *this*, Saab?" the salesman shouted.

"Yes, that, that," said Donat.

In front of him, stretched across the entire length of the shop, on the top of a multicolored thick rainbow flattened on the floor, raged a storm of autumn leaves. As soon as Donat looked at the storm, he felt a passionate protest. It was a protest against everything in the world, a protest that did not try to prove anything, a protest consisting of a protest.

The wind blew, the leaves fell off and started to fly, turning and knocking against each other, fluttering, shooting upwards, gliding, and diving. They did not care where they'd fall or what would happen to them next. They could float from edge to edge of a puddle, they could get crumpled and wet, they could even drown— big deal. They could land flat on a wet cool stone, get darker, fall apart—big deal. They could get tangled in the dirty-brown dying grasses, speed down the river to meet the sea, push against the knife of a bush, lie on sandstone with their surfaces coated by sand, stick to each other with mud, dissolve in it, become mud—big deal!

Is what *will* happen next most important? Well, it is, but a moment later it turns into it *was*, it becomes familiar, old, and boring. So the most important things are those particles of time when you are flying from the old to the new, and in this uncomfortable space in-between you experience true freedom.

"How many meters?" shouted the merchant.

"Ten," said Donat guessing. And later he was sorry that he did not buy all the falling leaves.

The merchant cut the fabric, wrapped it up, and continued to break open and send into the air semicircles of different colors, hoping that he would sell Donat something else. Still thinking about falling leaves, Donat imitated with his hand a flying leaf, which was about ready to cut into the ground, but helped by a complex gust of the wind, again, shot up into the air and higher, into the sky, and, lucky, prolonged its freedom. The merchant did not know what Donat was thinking about, and interpreted his gesture commercially, as a wish to pause on a black and gold fabric, seemingly made of tiny scales, which twinkled with many colors in the soft folds, as a gold fish twinkles when it is lit with a bright light.

"Italian stocking?" asked the dealer.

"Italian stocking?" repeated Donat who was observing the lucky free leaf.

Rushing to sell the stocking, the dealer ignored the question mark. He slyly cut what seemed right, united the gold fish with the windy falling leaves, and, bowing low to the ground, handed the purchase to the customer.

Surprised, Donat laughed, paid as much as the merchant asked, and took the packet outside, onto the hot street. He was walking, looking for a ricksha, thinking about falling leaves in Russia, recalling the Italian stocking, and wondering: What do I need it for?

9

Apparently, this is what I needed it for, Donat thought, getting off Polina and tying up his robe. So that in this village, about which I did not know anything just about half a year ago, this woman would give herself to me to get the Italian stocking from India. How horrifying it is that all our actions are always pregnant with consequences. Of course, looking back from the future, one sees that many actions are fruitless. But that only means that their consequences are still ripening, that every action has its own unknown period of gestation, and that this period cannot be always contained by the span of human life. I wonder what will be the consequences of what just happened? thought Donat, walking on creaking polyphonic floorboards and looking from time to time at Polina, who was still lying in bed.

She sat up and adjusted her dress. Then she touched her hair and rose as if she saw something interesting in the window. She sat for a while in silence, pretending to look at the falling leaves. Finally, she sighed:

"Very nice colors."

"Listen, Polina," said Donat. "There is a suitcase under the bed. Take it out and open it."

"Why should I look in your suitcase?"

As if she did not understand anything, but complying with his caprice, Polina pulled out the suitcase, threw the top back, and clapped her hands with joy.

"The girls told the truth! It shimmers, like a gold fish."

"Take it, the gold fish is yours."

"You're not kidding? Can I unfold it?"

She let the Italian stocking fall along her body. Her happy little eyes shone above multicolored tinges.

"And now we'll see what is behind the falling leaves," Donat said, interrupting the moment of her happiness, took her hand, and led her behind the curtain.

Polina looked and almost yawned. Such splendid colors hid only a writing table, files with papers, and shelves with books.

"My study," explained Donat.

His visitor only smiled and tenderly patted the tiny fish scales.

10

Vania loitered about his quiet house, which felt a little cold after being tidied up. A generously set table stretched across the spacious dining room. He sat down at the head of the table the way he'd sit with the guests later, pulled closer a bottle of cognac, unscrewed the cap, poured some liquor into a glass, ran his eyes around the empty chairs, smiled, shook his hair, winked, and moved his glass as if he were clinking it with everyone at the same time.

"Well, dear guests, let's drink to my sixtieth birthday!"

Perhaps the souls of the guests are really sitting there, on the empty chairs, thought Vania, crunching on an apple. I thought about them and they all got hiccups. He drank one more glass of cognac and moved a commanding gaze over the chairs.

Vania's thoughts were so keen, so full of power to command, that all the people about whom he thought at that moment were unexpectedly taken by terrible, almost convulsive hiccups.

The chairman of the village Soviet, a responsible stubborn fellow, who used to gallop through his vast lands all the time, from Monday to Sunday, even at twelve o'clock at night on New Year's Eve, suddenly began to jerk and almost fell off his horse.

"I told you not to stuff yourself," said school director's wife to her husband when he emitted a terrifyingly loud hiccup, but at the same moment she hiccuped even louder. The face of the director seemed offended because he did not even think of stuffing himself, but just followed a quick shot of vodka with a little bit of sauerkraut.

"What are you doing there?" asked Ninka, seeing that Lyoshka began to convulse even though he was lying not on her, but next to her.

Oh, hic, someone's remembering me, hic, thought the shepherd. He called his dog, showered his hated herd with terrible elaborate curses, furiously cracked his knout, and whipped the nearest miserable cow. In other words, he told the beasts that if they continued to slow him down, the other guests would drink and eat away everything at the party, and there would be nothing left for him.

"Hic," jerked Grisha-the-stove-maker, accidentally nicking the bricks, which had not set yet. Then he went berserk and with his feet knocked down a whole week's worth of work.

In a house across the street something else happened; as a result of the first hiccup, a necklace, which someone was trying on, fell down. The thread holding the beads together broke and they all irretrievably ran in different directions and hid in various places.

All the other invited people whom Vania had time to remember when he carefully looked at the chairs (mechanics with their milkmaid-wives, the medical assistant, three old women, the teacher, the post office worker, and the saleswoman)—all hiccuped dreadfully and in unison.

11

Alexandra ate two spoonfuls of sugar and her hiccups stopped. Polina, who was still next to her, hiccuped with frenzy, as if someone were strangling her. She was trying to scream, but was able to make only a single sound and someone began strangling her again. She refused the sugar because she knew a better remedy: to hold her breath and count to ten.

"You can hold it even to a thousand," Alexandra said with a smirk and returned to her position on the bed in front of the window.

The lace of the leaves intertwined with the lace of the sky. In the sky she saw her Donat. She dressed up for the Pshenichkas party already in the morning. She was going to these boring people only to see the one who, at one time in her sunny childhood, rode behind her on the horse, hugging her tenderly and protectively and helping her push soft branches of summer birches away from her face. She was going there to see Donat.

You're a bitch, Polina, Alexandra thought. You can go to hell with your Italian stocking! Well, just you wait, you viper! Now you'll learn something too. . . .

"Wait a minute," she said to the leaving figure. "I want to tell you something."

Polina's pancake face began to burn from curiosity.

"I accidentally heard a most interesting thing. You know how it is in the store: someone says something, another disagrees, the third ads something and so on."

She said it exactly like that: *and so on*. After *so on* she started laughing and her white marbles sparkled. Polina also laughed, supportively. It's always better to agree with such people, she thought, but inside she was on guard.

"Yesterday in the store Antonina called Lilka a prostitute. The Party chairman was in the store too, and he lashed out at Antonina. 'You should be ashamed,' he said, 'Lilka is an activist, a party member, a single mother; this is just dirty gossip; people like you should be hanged by the tongue or uprooted like weeds.' And then Antonina got mad. 'Eh, you son of a bitch,' she swore like a soldier, 'you dirty swindler, you stinking billy-goat, we

should uproot you like a weed, then we would have reasons to go to the store.' And she spat in his face. He
turned as red as a beet, opened his mouth and tried to
catch his breath. But Antonina kept going, 'You defend
Lilka because she is the only one willing to sleep with
you.' The chairman cursed her and ran outside. But
Antonina kept waving her hands as if she were giving a
speech from a lectern, and she was yelling without a
microphone so loudly that the lamp was swinging and
the windows were ringing. 'This librarian bitch,' she said,
'should be kicked out from everywhere; she's got either
syphilis or AIDS, that's why she is so sickly and frail.
I'm sure she has brought it from the city, from a library
convention. She should, bitch, spend more time with her
son, pay more attention to him and be kinder, but no,
she puts him up for five days in a care center so she can
walk the streets, pretending that she is doing propaganda
work. Her little Igor will soon be three years old, but he
can barely move his legs and arms. He walks, like a wind-
up doll, he is so pale, almost transparent, and does not
say anything, only mumbles like a mute, like an idiot.
And his teacher says that little Igor is an idiot, and he'll
remain a mental case, he'll go to a school for fools. All
the kids are mental cases now,' Antonina yelled to the
microphone made of her own fist. 'All are underfed,
underdressed, underloved, and undereducated; after
kindergartens for fools, all of them will go to schools for
fools, and then the biggest fools will go to universities
for fools. Children are our future, they say, which means
that the future Russia will be exclusively a country of
fools.' How do you like that?"

Alexandra stopped.

"So you're saying that the chairman ran outside?" Polina asked, starving for more details.

"Yes, he ran out, but that's not important."

"Why?" Polina almost squealed.

The white-eyed one laughed.

"Wait, don't squeal yet. Slow down. I see that you're nervous getting ready for today's party. Apparently, you had no opportunity to talk to well-informed women yet. Otherwise they would have told you that yesterday Antonina, in front of the entire village, announced through her loud speaker the names of all the men who slept with Lilka and who should be treated for syphilis or AIDS. So you should know," Alexandra went on, turning the eyes of an ancient Greek bust to Polina, "that your Vaniusha was among them too."

Polina clutched her left breast.

"I'll kill that monster!" she growled and ran outside.

12

"Wow-wow!" said Vania when he saw Polina.

"What wow-wow?" she asked, adjusting the new dress. "I see that you've already started, you swine."

"I did start," he said, relaxing. "And now I am trying to figure out whether it is you or whether a gold fish has floated in. What are you wearing?"

"Why?" she asked daringly, and placed her hands on her waist, like a prostitute.

"Because I heard that all the cheap tricks on Broadway got fired. I will call there and ask to get the plane ready as soon as possible."

"What plane?" Polina did not catch on.

"To take you to Broadway. You'll be the head cheap trick there."

Polina wagged her hip on purpose, the way it is done on Broadway.

"It's better to be the first on Broadway, than to get smeared with such shit."

"What shit?" Her husband's voice became more stern.

"Like you!" Polina screamed and wished she could smack him on his filthy mug with the flowers standing in a vase, scratch him with her nails until he bled, say everything she wanted, and then strangle him.

But on her way home from Alexandra, she decided to be quiet for the time being, to lie on the bottom, like a submarine. First of all, the flounder was insane, she could have mixed everything up and she could have lied. Besides, it's been enough excitement for today; she needs to save herself for the guests.

Wisely, Vania also kept silent. He guessed that it made no sense to continue finding faults with the new dress. But if he did continue, he would have soon expressed an opinion that it did not matter what dress you put on a pig—a pig is always a pig. He would have said that the new dress was too short and too snug, and despite all its sparkle, it only emphasized the faults or, more precisely, the absence of a figure. After that, he would have sternly demanded from her to take off that slutty dress, which shamelessly exaggerated everything: nipples on sagging breasts, belly button in a wobbly belly, and that mound under the belly, which Vania never in his life saw on his spouse even when she was naked because it was always covered with an overgrown bush of black hair. Therefore now, when the mound, covered with the dress, started protruding, Polina looked worse than naked.

Vania squeezed his lips, like a wet rag, into a mock-ingly-loathful grimace and, sprawling on his chair, he observed how his wife, twisting her hips, walked along the table and for no apparent reason kept adjusting what had been placed there well enough. With every step the hem of her short dress tried to crawl up and reveal her panties. In order not to show her underwear, after every step Polina bent over and pulled the hem down. She'd take a step, bend, and pull down. Take a step, bend, and pull down.

"Well, are you going to walk like that when the guests are here?" Vania could not restrain himself, even though he tried hard, and once he could not restrain himself, he kept rolling, "What a nasty thing you've put on. A dress like that is just right to entertain rednecks, pimps, and soldiers. It's a slutty dress. Shame and disgrace!"

"You're slutty yourself," said Polina, indifferent on the surface, but attentive inside, after she heard her husband's review of her dress.

Vania's reaction was not positive, but she was ready for that because Vania made no more sense of women's clothing than he did of, let's say, poetry. She was mainly interested in how exactly he would evaluate the dress. His opinion made her happy, like the best praise. Because why would a woman dress up if not to make all men want to have her?

13

Alexandra forgot Polina at once and wept without tears over her own failed love. Donat's capitulation to Polina, to the dumb porky milkmaid, had shaken her as much as, perhaps, the fall of angels after the rebellion of Lucifer had once shaken God.

Perhaps, asked the inquisitive mind of the failed historian, there is no history at all, and everything that happened before, will actually happen or is happening right now? Perhaps Lucifer rebelled not sometime in the past, but today, the angels are falling right now, and Donat is one of those angels?

All the guests arrived at the Pshenichkas long ago. The village could already hear songs pleasing to the drunken Russian heart; the stove-setter had already begun to fight with the shepherd; Lyoshka smacked Ninka on the face and kept pinching Polina under the new dress almost in view of her husband; saliva had already dribbled involuntarily from the flaccid mouth of Vania Pshenichka while he recklessly kept shaking his hair and making eyes at all the milkmaids; the medical assistant had already danced as many times as she wanted to; the director of the school had already explained the methodology of educating fools and peacefully slept with his head surrounded by bottles and plates; Donat, in a drunken depression, had already abandoned all those repugnant people and was walking, unstoppable, like a tank, through the dark forest; the chairman, half-drunk, had jumped on his horse and galloped away to watch the trees grow in the forest; and the three old women had managed to run away to be the first to tell what happened during the birthday party. And behind everything that had happened, that is happening, and that will happen, hid the invisible rebellious Lucifer.

Meanwhile, Alexandra, torturing herself by resurrecting the best moments of her life, continued sitting in front of the invisible sky and the invisible leaves.

14

After the first meeting with Donat she did not see him for a long time. From the school girls who came to the store, she learned what took place when Donat, apparently drunk and lacking the skill, tried to ride a colt. With a broken hand and rib he was taken to the regional hospital. He stayed there a while and returned in a cast. And then he came to the store again, said his complex *Good morning*, and again she smiled cheerfully.

"Are you getting better, Donat Vasilievich?"

"I am," said the teacher. "And what have *you* been doing?"

"I missed you, Donat Vasilievich."

He looked into the white marble of her eyes.

"Then why didn't you drop by?"

"Because it's awkward, Donat Vasilievich."

He laughed.

"It's awkward throughout our entire life. Only time when it's not awkward is when we're laid in the grave."

"True," hoarsely said a manual laborer, who was moving boxes in the back of the store.

"I'd rather you came to see me," Alexandra said tenderly. "I will treat you to tea and a cake."

"Why tea?" suddenly asked an old man, who had been sleeping half the day on the window sill. "After tea, a man is not a man. Tea weakens you and puts you to sleep. Look at me; I had some tea, and what? Give him some vodka and you're in business."

"There's no business without vodka," wheezed the invisible manual laborer. "Without vodka Russia will not survive."

Donat put five roubles on the counter.

"Please give me a bottle of *Extra* and some glasses."

She handed him four glasses, nested in each other, covered with dust and straw, and she put the bottle on the counter.

"And use the change for some *Russian* cheese," added Donat.

She cut four pieces of cheese, then bread, and put them together into sandwiches. Donat separated the glasses, shook out the straw used as packing material, pulled off the bottle's cap, and poured the vodka evenly in each glass. Nothing could have been more clear, but the other three did not budge; instead, they attentively, affectedly waited for a word.

"Please," said Donat.

The old man quacked loudly and, like a youth, jumped deftly from the window sill in the direction of the counter. The manual laborer approached in a huge mass. Alexandra gracefully nodded, accepting the glass handed to her. Dust and rubbish floated on the vodka's surface, but for some reason, she liked it.

"Let's drink to Russia's survival," said Donat, raising his glass.

The glasses met with a series of clangs. Then, with pleasure, the four drank their vodka to Russia's survival. In silence they chased the vodka with *Russian* cheese.

"Good cheese," mumbled the old man.

"I'll get some more," Alexandra said and cut several thick long slices off a head of cheese.

The old man quacked with delight again, "Who would have thought, who would have guessed, but this party is the best!"

"What kind of a party is it with only one bottle," said Donat as he started rummaging in his money purse.

The huge paw of the manual laborer grabbed his thin wrist.

"An advance," he said hoarsely, ready to drink away his future.

The door opened and a woman came in. The manual laborer was already walking towards her and the woman disappeared behind his large body. The heavy iron lock rattled. They had another drink without a toast.

"The *Russian* cheese is always good," said Alexandra, flushed from the vodka. "The *Soviet* brand," she went on, "stays on the shelf, but everybody buys this one."

"You look at the *Soviet* brand and you think of national minorities," wheezed the follower of nationalism, hiding under the disguise of the manual laborer.

The old man extracted five roubles from his pocket and slapped it on the counter.

"Here, auntie, that's all I have."

Alexandra swept the five rouble note to the floor with a new bottle.

"My treat," she said.

The old man slammed his forehead against the counter and started crying loudly with sobs, pulling the hemisphere of his grey hair with his dirty twisted fingers.

"Brykov has had enough!" said the dictator, looking authoritatively at the manual laborer.

The manual laborer, promoted to the rank of enforcer, used his two mighty dirty fingers to lift the old man by his collar to the ceiling and to carry the unruly party-goer through the dark fissure of the back door. Then, he returned and looked at Donat with the eyes of a rabid dog and an executioner.

"Brykov's party is over," he wheezed.

Donat threw his unfinished glass at the dimly shining lampshade. There was a sound of broken glass. And silence.

It was quiet inside. It was quiet on the street. It was quiet in the houses. It was quiet in the forest. In the quiet, average, and god-forsaken Russia an old man was sleeping quietly on the sacks, and a teacher, a saleswoman, and a manual laborer, drunk as skunks, swayed in silence.

15

Alexandra felt sick. She started walking. Stumbled over boxes. Fell down. She crawled through the crack of the back door and rested next to Brykov on the sacks. She threw up and fell into a heavy sleep.

A man was bending over her.

"Who are you?" she asked the man and, astonished, realized that she was not laying on the sacks, but in her own bed, undressed.

"You're alive, thank God," said the man.

"Donat?" She could not believe her ears. "But how did I? . . . Oh my God—Donat!"

"Drink," quietly said Donat, handing her a glass of vodka. "You'll feel better."

She drank, obediently.

"Are you better?"

Music was starting inside her.

"Drink some more," said Donat.

She drank some more.

"I was also drunk."

"And Brykov, and Brykov," she said and laughed like a bride.

"Listen." Donat bent over even more. "What happened to your eyes?"

She laughed. Stupid little Donat. What happened to my eyes? What happened to all my life? Whose fault is it? Is it the fault of that grey-haired American woman from the huge sparkling tourist bus, who gets restless from having nothing to do, from having too much money, from visiting too many countries, museums, and restaurants? Since she knows that she'll die soon, she is constantly in a hurry! On the day of the accident she suffered from the most terrible Russian heartburn and could barely move her legs. The others waited for her patiently in the bus to go to Petrozavodsk; they hated her, but they smiled to her with their false smiles, smiles of overstuffed emptiness. It took her so long to get to the bus from the hotel that the delayed bus drove through the city much faster than the street signs permitted.

"Why?" Alexandra kept opening and closing her eyes. "You've never slept with someone who had white eyes?"

He caressed her hair.

"I fell in love with your eyes."

"What!" Alexandra went crazy. "Hand me my robe," she said.

He handed her the robe and turned away. She lowered her legs to the floor, put the robe on, and tied it up.

"I'd better be going," said Donat.

She ran to the door before him, put the hook on, and turned to Donat.

"Am I so unattractive?"

"You are beautiful!" he said—sincerely and untruthfully at the same time.

"So?" she asked, trembling and not believing, but hoping blindly.

Donat embraced her sharp shoulders and touched her cheek with his lips in her first masculine, momentary and eternal, tender and deadly, last kiss. Then, he lifted the hook and went out forever.

Alexandra threw herself on the bed and began sobbing without tears into a pillow. Her legs, sticking out from under her robe, were naked, bony, sprinkled with rust, and not needed by anyone.

A Veranda
for Showers

1

Edward found himself in a situation he had been in before; again, he got thoroughly shaken in an old bus going stop-by-stop from San Jose to Coconut Shore. The bus stopped again, this time in the middle of a jungle, not far from food stalls. Edward walked by dried fruits, nuts, sweets and other things he would have trouble naming. Finally, he asked where he could buy beer. Someone pointed to a corner of a structure barely protruding from the thicket. He approached the structure, entered and stopped in front of a makeshift counter. Behind the counter and under an awning made of reeds, was a yard. In the middle of the yard stood an oinking and staggering piglet and in the shadow of a tree lay a sleepy dog; it opened its eyes for a moment, did not notice anything unusual about the elderly man looking around, and returned to its half-dreams. Edward shouted out a couple of words. A second later, he heard nearby youthful, resonant voices and, as unexpectedly as an explosion, an indescribably beautiful eighteen-year-old girl appeared in front of him. She merrily looked Edward over, smiled divinely and handed him a bottle of cold beer. Another, younger girl appeared, followed by another, and then by one more. All these young nymphs were elegant and gracious, with sophisticated, intelligent faces. Where is their mother? thought Edward and at the same moment the mother, thin, beautiful, and young, looking like the girls' older sister, stepped into the yard. And the father?

The father also appeared, and his face was understanding and good. Edward asked for a second bottle. The girls, the mother and the father, the piglet and the dog, the wood of the counter, and the beer bottle, filled Edward's soul with a strong premonition that here he would be happier than he had ever been anywhere else. He passionately wished to stay, to marry one of the girls, no matter which one, and to become a friend of the mother and the father. Everything in the world came together, everything promised an ideal continuation. . . . He heard the honking of the bus ordering him to return to his tedious, former life. His fingers squeezed the beer bottle so hard that, had he been just a little more angry at everything that kept him from being free, they would have broken it. Ashamed to look back at the abandoned paradise, he was returning, his hand uncut, to his former life. . . .

A stewardess with a red moon on her forehead woke him up.

"We'll be landing soon," she said, looking at him with eyes as large as half of her face. "Please, fasten your belt."

In the plane's window, either far away or so near that you could touch them, shone the striking white peaks of the Himalayas. Edward was already anticipating the cool air, smelling of snow and flowers, but as soon as the plane stopped, the temperature inside quickly rose and, leaving the cabin behind, the passengers entered hell. Bathing in his own sweat, Edward got into the oven of the taxi and asked the driver to switch on the air-conditioner. The driver turned to him the black shrubs of his never-shaven face, crowned at the top with a soiled turban, not washed for a long time.

"In our region," he said with pride resembling patriotism, "we don't need artificial cooling. On the contrary," he added through his nape, "we freeze here quite often."

Edward still hoped for the cool hall of the hotel and a room with air-conditioning. I'll enter the foyer, he planned, and at first I'll ignore the desk. At first I'll sit down in a comfortable armchair close to a cold stream of air and the splashing drops of a gurgling fountain, and I'll sit there as long as I want. His hope wilted instantly in the stifling, steamy air of the hotel *Republic*, in the nauseating smell of its old carpets and in the futile squeaking of the ceiling fan. Edward walked up to the desk and rested his wet elbows on it.

"Are you absolutely sure that you reserved a room in the *Republic* and not in some other hotel?" asked a thin, but pot-bellied manager with a dark, nervous face.

"My secretary made the reservations."

The manager again looked through the papers piled up on a small table.

"Your secretary mixed something up. Sir, I have to disappoint you; we have no vacant rooms."

"No vacant rooms," repeated Edward, beginning to panic under the impact of all his misfortunes. "How about some other hotel? This one or another—what's the difference, I am going to be here only two nights. What really matters is that the room has air-conditioning."

"Sir, all the hotels are packed. Our city is hosting an important event, an annual agricultural fair. You probably know about it. Didn't you come for the fair?"

"No," said Edward. "Not for the fair. I am here on business. With the firm *Rao and Sons*."

The face of the manager began to dance to the music of some complex feelings caused by Edward's answer; then, it remembered about air-conditioning. . . . The balloon belly on the thin body shook in a spasm of controlled laughter, and the mouth let loose a nightmare:

"Sir, in our city you will not discover even one room with air-conditioning. Rooms with artificial cooling can be found only in a few large enterprises, among which, you'll be happy to know, is *Rao and Sons*. By the way, perhaps they mixed up your reservations? Why don't you call them?"

All Edward reached at the firm was the answering machine.

"Of course. It's late. Everybody there went home," the manager's face expressed not only his scorn for the firm's workers, but also his compassion, sympathy and sorrow for Edward and his need to make peace with fate. "There is a solution," he continued, challenging fate. "I could put you temporarily in the vacant room on the roof. It will be, of course, pretty warm, but the shower, the fan, and your fortitude will help you lower the temperature to quite bearable degrees."

Edward's smile did not come out right; it was distorted by the time difference between India and New York, by the lack of sleep after the long flight across the Atlantic, and by the prospect of returning to the fiery furnace of the street to look for a hotel with a vacancy.

"Fine," he nodded. "I'll take the room on the roof."

"Sir," said the manager quietly, after he finished registering Edward. "Someone in town may tell you that in that room something happened. Please, do not pay much attention to such rumors."

"Did someone die there from the heat?"

"We rarely have hot weather here. And the heat today is a record high."

"Then what happened?" Edward wanted to know.

"Don't worry. You'll be fine."

Edward followed a bellboy. Shaking, squealing, shuddering, and screeching, the elevator took them to the top of the hotel. They ascended one more flight of weak, almost temporary stairs. There, in the condensed heat, was a lone door without a lock. The door opened and they were hit by a wave of heat as in a sauna. The bellboy pointed his finger in various directions:

"Sir, there's an iron roof all around you."

2

The night passed in an agonizing insomnia. From time to time, Edward would get up, soak his sheets under the warm shower, lie back in bed wrapped in the evaporating moisture, and when the sheets were dry, he would get up again and drag himself to the shower stall. He fell asleep only before dawn. But not for long. He was awakened by knocking. He opened the door. Nobody was there. He slammed the door, annoyed. The draft accelerated the door's speed and ended in a deafening thunder that probably woke up all the hotel guests. Edward moved from the door on tiptoes and approached the open window.

A flat roof of an adjacent house stretched below. Someone was building on the roof a simple brick addition, perhaps a small kitchen—an assumption confirmed by weak smoke from the temporary stove. A man was crouching in the midst of building materials, chopping wooden boards into small pieces. A heavy woman came out on the roof and gave an order in a sharp voice. The man nodded, dropped his axe, slipped his thin body into the addition and vanished. The woman looked around, yawned, and left, too.

Edward wanted to get back to bed, but he was detained at the window by the morning air filled with birds and flowers. Then, the servant appeared again, but now he was one floor below, on a cement veranda that was protected from the rain by an awning and from the eyes of neighbors and pedestrians by a high wall. Potted flowers stood on top of the wall. The dark-skinned, lean body of the servant was struggling with two buckets of water. He was walking towards a dark-blue barrel.

How odd, remembered Edward, yesterday there was no barrel there. Yesterday, when I looked through the window, I saw on the veranda a rattan table and several armchairs. In such a heat, I thought, nobody would want to sit on the veranda. But it must be wonderful to relax there during the season of south-western monsoons. I know how good it is to sprawl in an armchair with a glass of whisky or rum and to watch a wall of water falling down three steps away and crashing onto the ground. Noise, cool splashes of water, the wind and the quivering contours of a tree blurred by the rain. . . .

During such moments, his memory occasionally painted two girls under the tree. Physically, they were almost adolescent, but their behavior—cowering under a tree during a storm—made them look more like scared little girls. They stood there deafened and blinded, frightened by the crumpled black clouds, while the threads of the pouring rain and the needles of lightning kept sewing the earth and the sky together with the speed of an insane *Singer*. Edward cut sharply towards the shore, convinced them to get into the boat and took them to the city dock. The shower seemed to have undressed one of the girls; her light dress turned transparent from the water. Edward, then a twenty-year-old student, kept fighting his own eyes and dreamed that the dock would be a hundred miles away. . . .

The servant placed one of the buckets on the floor, lifted the other with effort, and turned it over above the barrel. The water jumped out of the bucket, like a big shimmering fish. The servant disappeared, but soon appeared again, and the scene, ending with the fish, was repeated many times. Edward endured the boredom of these repetitions because he hoped that the barrel would be finally filled up and a new scene would begin. Perhaps this new scene will be even more boring than the previous one—let's say, the water will just shine in the barrel and at best everything will be enlivened by a bird coming to have a drink—but we all make peace with the present only by hoping against hope that the future scenes from our lives will be more exciting.

It seemed as if the servant lived all his life with lowered eyes. However, if at that moment his eyes rebelled and soared above the horizon, towards the window of the hotel, he would have noticed there a foreigner cut at the waist by the window sill. And if he looked a little bit longer, he would have noted the whiteness of the bloated, flabby body, unusual in these dark-skinned regions, a pot-belly, a balding forehead with graying remains of hair, and partially-tinted glasses (without which, because of his advanced shortsightedness, Edward could get around only in his shower and, obviously, in his dreams).

Finally, the barrel was filled to the rim. The servant vanished for good and the birds that always notice everything looked askance with the shiny beads of their eyes at the shiny circle of water. The servant reappeared on the roof and continued to chop the wood. Somewhere, a radio began playing an endless mournful melody.

Edward had an appointment at the firm at nine. If he were more reasonable, he would have gone back to bed, but he continued to stand at the window. Interesting, how will the woman wash; will she keep her sari on or take it off? The latter seemed more natural, but as a man who traveled all over the world, Edward acquired the right to claim that half of the women on earth wash their bodies without undressing. Anyhow, it wouldn't hurt to spy on this intimate scene and take a few photographs. Edward closed the dusty blinds, leaving a crack about the size of his face.

Something moved on the veranda. The familiar heavy-set woman was walking towards the barrel; she was carrying a naked baby girl on her hip, tossing her to and fro like a skiff on the ocean waves. Then she lifted the girl above the barrel—Edward took a photograph—and dipped her in water. The girl started to cry and kick her feet, but the woman put her down on the cement, lathered her body, washed the soap off, picked the girl up, and carried her away. The crying, calming down, withdrew into the house and again the mournful melody began to rule over all the sounds of the street.

Now, as long as nothing is happening on the veranda, we can provide a slightly boring, but necessary explanation why Edward was inseparable from his camera and his telephoto lens. Working in the export department, he was frequently sent to different countries to sign contracts for delivery of agricultural machinery, and occasionally he had to deal with warranty complaints. Most of the complaints came from the third world countries, where the machinery, sold by Edward's corporation, was ruined by poor service. It was useful to attach to the report of warranty violations photographs showing the broken part, the deficient service depot, the condition of the unit that was not serviced properly, a dirty filter or rarely changed oil. But besides that, there were much more interesting reasons for Edward's and his camera's inseparable coexistence. From time to time, he would find himself in places, about which the tourist agencies knew nothing. He would photograph something unusual there and he would send particularly interesting photographs to journals. Among those that got published were children sleeping on the back of a gigantic buffalo barely sticking out of a river, a farmer terribly mutilated by a tiger, and a man, grown in a jug, with a huge head and a body of a dwarf. Edward made enlargements of his best photographs and hung them on the walls of his living room; this way, another use was added to their regular decorative purpose—there was something to talk about even with the most boring guests.

3

A white flower blossomed on the veranda; it was a twelve-year-old girl. Perhaps older, thought Edward. All these slender Indian girls look much younger than most of their peers in America. She was wearing a white nightgown that almost swept the cement floor. She approached the barrel, dipped her hands and ponytails in it and, resting her chin on the metal rim, began to splash the water delicately. Edward's powerful zoom lens brought the girl as close as three feet. He kept pushing her back until flowerpots and a large bird, sitting between them and attracted by the water, appeared in the frame. The shutter clicked and the beautiful moment wasn't lost among other moments, relentlessly arriving from the future. Then, the girl stepped away from the barrel, bent down, grabbed the bottom of her gown, stood up straight, lifted her arms, and holding her white gown in one hand, as if it were a white flag, she surrendered her naked, thin body to his camera.

What am I doing, old idiot? I am a vice director of a department of an international corporation, I've been married for thirty years, I have three married daughters, and yet I am shamelessly spying from my window on a naked bathing Indian Lolita, and I am even secretly taking pictures of her. What will I do with these pictures? I won't send them to a journal and I won't hang them in my living room. . . . What would my wife say?

The girl abandoned the veranda only to return with a large dipper. She drowned it in the barrel, lifted it with difficulty, bent slightly under its weight and poured on herself a little torrential shower. We've been assured, thought Edward, that time moves only forward. But then, why are there so many ways—books, movies, photos, memory—why are there so many ways to return to what had already happened? From now on, this young Indian girl, whenever I desire, will obediently bend, like a young tree standing against the wind. The shower of everything men throw on women will drop with pitiless force on her weak shoulders. And that melody will again mourn her whenever I wish so.

The girl scooped the water again, placed the dipper next to her, crouched, began to lather her body, then spilled several more showers; after that the veranda became empty. He should have returned to bed and somehow slept until it was time to go to work, but anticipating some continuation he remained at the window.

A street. White cows. They are just resting. Or walking slowly. Or chewing a piece of newspaper. Rickshas without passengers. They push wheel against wheel and, waiting for clients, exchange words. A boy-servant is running across the street with twenty cups of tea. . . .

Emerging from under the cement overhang and following the wet tracks left by the first girl, an adolescent girl entered the veranda. He must have imagined what was happening on the street after he saw the first girl. Most likely, he got lost for a few years in a forgotten fragment of his life. Later, he returned to this hotel, stood at dawn at the window, and saw how the same, but now more mature girl walked up to the barrel with water. She stretched, lifted her head, and looked straight at Edward. He jumped away from the window and then carefully peeked through the crack between the flapping blinds. The girl was lifting the bottom of her nightgown. She didn't notice me, he thought, and continued to take pictures. Above the knees, even higher. . . . And then, as if somebody made a grave error—pulled the wrong string—the curtain fell, hiding the stage, and the actress, like a frightened bird, took wing and flew away. . . .

The street. The white cows. The boy-servant is running with twenty empty cups. . . .

The veranda was filled—perhaps even overfilled— by the familiar heavy woman in a sari. She walked up to the barrel. Or perhaps he was lost again, perhaps now he was lost for twenty years or so? This is what the girl turned into. What kind of life is it, why is it going on— just to turn a treasure into a barrel of lard? Casting a

sidelong look at the hotel's window and letting him know
that he was seen, the woman put her hands in the water,
splashed herself several times, turned her wet face to
Edward (and to those who will see her in his photo al-
bum), sharply turned around, and dived into the depths
lurking under the roof.

A pink ray of light touched the bulbous roof of the
building on the other side of the street; the delicately
colored finger of the sun was announcing to those who
wanted to see it that soon the city would be assailed by
excruciating heat. The birds will fly away and hide from
it. Where? In shadows unknown to humans. The flowers will quickly age from the heat; many will age irrevo-
cably. And the heat will make the air so sweaty, so smelly,
and so dusty that one will do better running away from
it. But where can one hide from the air? Unable to escape the heat, people will habitually continue doing everything they've been taught by centuries. The astrolo-
gers and palm readers, the idlers and the poor, dogs,
goats, children, vendors of sweets and spices, and the
sellers of sandalwood sticks and pan (when people chew
it, they look like vampires: their mouths are filled with
red saliva, frequent and plentiful spits splash the walls
and the sidewalks, and the streets resemble a movie set
prepared for the filming of a massacre of demonstra-
tors)—all will sit down, looking like animated, noisy tree
stumps. Trucks, buses, and cars will speed by, roaring
and covering them in dust. Barely touching the hot
ground, bicycles and three-legged carriages will roll, carrying passengers in blindingly-white clothes. An elephant will stomp, a camel will sway, a bull will ram its
way through, and a buffalo will wobble, passing by.

A servant with a floor rag joylessly animated the veranda. Edward closed the window more tightly, got into bed and thought that under the quiet surface of his life, normal and even successful on the outside, everything was muddled up by anxiety and doubt, and to look even deeper inside was terrifying because for many years that space had been inhabited by an ugly creature called failure.

4

His marriage was considered successful only by the number of years he spent with his wife. Obviously, a transparent dress is not the best reason for marriage. Even though it was so transparent, it placed such an opaque veil around the girl's soul that Edward finally began to see through it only when his first daughter was born. After graduating from their colleges, his daughters turned into cold and shallow Philistines, found themselves exactly the same mates, and remembered their father only during holidays or when they needed him (that is, when they needed his money). He should not have given up then, long ago; he should have brought them up with the same strictness, with which he was brought up. Instead, he abandoned them to be devoured by teenage friends, liberal ideas, and stupefying television.

His profession, international trade, Edward selected not with his heart, but heeding the advice of other people and taking into account financial advantages. He understood too late that every job should engage some unique talent, that is, the inborn talent to do something better than the others. Was he given any talents? Was he given a talent to feel differently than other people? He did not have enough courage to say *yes*. But if he answered *no*, at least he could ask another question: Why was he sometimes able to notice the moments when unexpectedly and mysteriously *everything came together* in such a way that he experienced a feeling possibly reserved only for those living in paradise? If someone asked Edward to describe such a feeling, he probably would not find precise words; instead, he would illustrate this state—this *everything came together*—with situations, but without hope that his interlocutor would ever feel the same thing. Music and feminine beauty often played an important part in those situations. It was not the physical beauty pushed on men by women, but the fleeting and mysterious one: the maddening bow of a head; the wave of unearthly origin suddenly flooding a face; or the trembling of a curl on a neck that melts, like a white candle, and its hot wax drips, searing your heart.

Perhaps everything in the world used to *come together* all his life, but for the first time he clearly noticed this condition when as a thirty-year-old father he sat at a school concert. The orchestra, which included his daughter, played a tune by Mozart. The tune was beautiful, but it was marred by an erratic performance (nevertheless, the parental enthusiasm made a tremendous success out of it). Bored, Edward scrutinized the musicians and his eyes stopped at a girl, gracefully leaning towards her cello. She wore a black silk dress and her shiny long hair rhythmically, like ocean waves, rolled over her instrument. It seemed that she trembled all over—from the music, from being so young or from being in love with someone. *Here is a girl*, he thought and in that moment the externally common schoolgirl suddenly grew up to the sky and squashed him with her future. It seemed as if the abyss of all the emotions of all those men who would ever fall in love with her showed in her instantly, simultaneously, in explosively dangerous concentration. . . .

Another time, he stopped his car at a light. Listening to baroque music, he suddenly discovered in his rearview mirror a cute little face. Darting glances from side to side, the girl was retouching her eyelashes; after that she opened her tender lips and made them even more desirable with lipstick and pencil. Then, after she put the cosmetics in her purse, her face became serious and she got lost in thought. At that moment, time seemed to stop and Edward understood that *everything came together*: the old classical music, and the pretty thoughtful face, and the fat white clouds lazily sprawled above Paris, and the girl's romantic recollection, which he seemed to have perceived. . . .

And once, on a cloudy and windy day in autumn, Edward was slowly strolling through a park. It began to snow; the snow was prickly and tiny and it rustled against the dry leaves. Soon, this rustling sound formed a rhythm and a melody, composed by some higher power and expressing Edward's longing for that unique woman he was unable to meet. The park grew dull from unexpected tears that resembled the tears shed during the final farewell to the dream of living through great love. And, unable to move forward, Edward fell into a bittersweet daze. . . .

Let's say he knew that he had a talent, but how could he find a practical application for it, what business could it relate to? There are, indeed, such strange talents that the society either does not need them or their bearers cannot not figured out how to bring them to society and make them popular commodities.

What a curse! thought Edward. Why did he always choose paths that turned wrong? Why after he discovered his mistake, did he continue to move in the wrong direction? Why wasn't he resolute enough to drop everything and throw himself head first at the hindrances of impassable roads?

5

Again, he did not know whether he was able to fall asleep or simply fell into a daydream, but, nevertheless, he got up with the alarm clock, arrived at the firm exactly at nine, just in time for the beginning of the talks, and then, the entire day, he kept swallowing strong Indian tea with milk and tried to stay as close as he could to the refreshing stream of the air-conditioner that sprinkled him with tiny sharp drops smelling of ozone and ammonia. After he finished his business, he dropped by the director's office.

"Would you like me to get you a car?" a pretty secretary asked him. "Will you wait a little? Mister Rao went to the bank, but he'll be back shortly. Would you like more tea?"

How funny the words sound on her lips. A typical Indian pronunciation mixed with an Oxford accent. She must have studied in England. Perhaps I should invite her to a bar? But he knew what would follow next; looking at the playful *old chap*, this cute Indian woman would widely open her olive eyes and thus would humiliate him. He does not need to get burned for any reason.

"Thank you; I'll manage without a car."

He went onto the street and looked around. An empty carriage was rolling by.

"Hey, babudji!"

The ricksha approached.

"Sit down, Saab. Where to, Saab?"

"To some restaurant where it's cool."

The ricksha driver did not understand; he heard an order like that first time in his life. From his point of view all the restaurants were much cooler than the street, but he nodded confidently and rushed to an expensive restaurant where he had a chance to make some money for bringing a foreign customer. And now, Edward and everyone else rolls down the dusty and noisy street. He is different than all the others within a mile, and everyone turns to look at him. The spokes sparkle, the dust gleams, like silver. Everything else—the walls, the clothes, the road—is white.

In the dark elongated restaurant, resembling the inside of a pencil-box, it was, of course, not cool, but there was a fountain and a draft was ruffling clothing, hair, and tablecloths. Edward sat next to the fountain. Weak rivulets flew up from the perimeter of a round fountain bowl; they bumped into each other in the center above the bowl and fell down on the golden figure of some Indian god.

After ordering beer and food, Edward said:

"I heard that in the hotel *Republic* something happened. . . ."

"Again?" exclaimed the waiter.

"A year ago," clarified Edward. "What happened there a year ago?"

"A foreigner was murdered there. Yes, with an axe."

Edward lingered in the restaurant for a long time. Then, he thought he should get up, walk out on the street, and drive. No, not to the hotel. So where? In this country people either go to the movies or wander around town.

He went out on the heat-breathing street and called a ricksha:

"To the movie theater."

The previous two sleepless nights, many bottles of beer, the food in the restaurant, and the swinging of the carriage lulled him into deep sleep. Loud shouts woke him up. He saw a crowd behind a fence. Look at that, thought Edward, even the mounted police is here. There are only men in the crowd. It must be grass hockey or rugby. In such heat? No kidding, these are truly children of the sun. The men sit at the stadium, while their women are raped in the backyards of their houses by the rays of the sun. The ricksha went on. It passed by a poster announcing *Show-Show-Show*. Below the poster was a drawing of a skeleton and under it small letters in Hindi. Further down the street, above the entrance to a tarpaulin tent, Edward noticed another similar poster.

"What is that, babudji?"

"Magic, sir."

"Stop here."

"Sir, how about the movies?"

No, today he will do without sleazily pretty lovers, singing and dancing on a flowering meadow on the background of the snowy Himalayas. They kiss once and sing. They kiss again, and sing again. And even before they begin kissing, they hold hands and sing. No, today he'll try the magic.

6

Inside the tent stood rows of wooden benches and a stage crudely put together. Its center was covered by the curtain made from white sheets, with a charcoal drawing of a skeleton on it. The tarpaulin of the tent had seen better days, but with the help of patches made of any available fabric it continued its life beyond the boundaries of old age. The patches were attached to the tarpaulin with string and resembled fat frogs warming themselves in the sun. In the holes that were still unpatched, the sun was playing with the dust.

Edward was approached by a man in a uniform quite similar to the uniforms of attendants serving tea in state institutions, but distinguished from those despised ones by the silvery ribbons around the hat and the sleeves. The man saluted like a policeman:

"Your seat is in the third row."

After a short wait, the same attendant ascended the stage. The audience became silent. Street sounds came closer. The sheets of the curtain parted and on the stage, in place of the charcoal skeleton, stood a short man with popping eyes, a wide face, a big belly, and a large mustache; he wore tails with a red bow-tie and carried a staff. He moved his eyes across the audience, lifted his staff, and pointed to someone. A slender boy, perhaps eight years old, found his way to the stage, sat on its edge, and started kicking his naked feet. The magician shouted, "Ah-hah!" and a potato appeared in his hand. He threw the potato to the boy, who caught it deftly and placed it next to him on the stage. The magician shouted "Ah-hah!" again and in his hand he was holding an onion; again, he threw it to the boy. After the onion came a cu-

cumber, a glass of water, luminescent lamp, a walking
stick with a handle, matches, and an axe. The boy caught
all the objects and placed them in a row on the stage.
The magician, much thinner now, started poking his staff
in all the objects, explaining something in detail.

Bored, Edward looked around and noticed in the corner of the stage something like a large tube pointing its
round aperture at the audience. Perhaps the skeleton is
in the tube? Or perhaps it is a skeleton-shooting can-
non? At that moment, the music started playing; the boy
picked up the potato; the magician touched it with his
staff, and the staff burst in a smoking flame. The onion
ignited the lamp; the cucumber lit the match. . . .

Huddling and laughing nervously, rubbing his knees
against themselves, the boy was sitting on an iron plate
connected to electricity, and the magician, stepping on
the other plate, kept touching the boy with different objects, closing the electric circuit. Edward felt a shiver as
if his body also closed this circuit, but he shivered not
because of the boy, but because the cold stream of air in
the offices of *Rao and Sons* blew on him for too long.

After a short intermission, the curtain moved again
and from behind it an old grey-haired woman in a bright,
spring-colored sari appeared on the stage. She turned,
like a model, and walked to the other end of the tube;
the magician shouted; inside the tube something resembling a camera shutter closed and opened, and in the
opening everyone could see a woman. Her figure was
slowly dissolving as if she were stepping deeper and
deeper in water. Then there appeared some drawing,
something resembling a grid . . . and suddenly in the
hole stood the skeleton. It flapped its hands and legs,
moved its jaws, and twirled its skull.

Edward remembered his camera, took a picture of the skeleton and realized that in one day, in an almost frightening sequence, he caught on film a baby, a girl, a teenager, a woman, an old crone, and, finally, a skeleton. He started thinking what could be behind such coincidence and how he could name such a selection of photographs, but the magician again clapped his hands, the bones turned into flesh, and the woman came out of the tube. She dropped a curtsey to the audience and left the stage.

The magician took the axe in his hands, stepped towards Edward and, with a gesture, invited him to come up on the stage. Edward, also with a gesture, declined his invitation. The magician said something and all the viewers burst into laughter.

"He says," a neighbor leaned towards Edward, "that after the incident in the *Republic* foreigners are afraid of axes."

Edward was offended, but not too much. His experience from travels to various places, especially to developing countries, taught him long before that the nature of people and whole nations is universally the same: nobody really likes the rich, the powerful, or foreigners. Edward reacted to the joke in the same way that all others, ridiculed by comedians, react; he forced himself to laugh.

That was the end of the spectacle. Edward went outside with the crowd and stopped absentmindedly. He did not want to go to the hotel. The spring-colored bright sari rustled by as if next to him rustled something resembling deliverance. Edward jumped out of emptiness, caught up with the woman, and walked close behind.

"Excuse me, please, for one moment."

The woman turned her head and stopped. The entire street was watching them.

"I was at your show. I would like to ask you one question."

"How I turn into a skeleton?"

"I think I figured that out. What do you know about the incident? A year ago? In the hotel *Republic*?"

She recoiled and started walking fast, lifting with her legs the bright colors as if she obstinately and forcibly herded in front of her everything good that happened in her life.

7

"Someone is waiting for you," said the manager. "The elderly gentleman on the left, on the sofa."

Edward looked at the sofa on the left. The elderly gentleman was reading a newspaper.

"What does he want?"

"He said he would like to see the man who occupies the room on the roof."

"How long has he been waiting?"

"About two hours."

Edward wiped his wet forehead with his sleeve.

"You've got a real cooker here. Why don't you install air-conditioning?"

"Sir, we often freeze here because the Himalayas are so close."

"Well, I think I'll go to my room."

"Sir, you forgot about the gentleman."

Edward pretended he did not hear. He went to the elevator and stepped inside. Behind the thick metal grate, the elderly gentleman started descending. Once in his room, Edward immediately tore off his clothes and threw them on the floor. Wet and white, like an egg just taken out of water, he walked over the soaked clothes smelling of his body. He pulled off the sheets, dry and crisp as a bouquet forgotten on the fireplace. He stepped under the thin warm rain, the sheet thrown across his shoulder like a Greek tunic. The streams warmed up and soon became hot.

He lay down, swathed in the sheets. Someone quietly knocked on the door. Strange thing a fan is. It hangs like a spider on the ceiling. The spider is crawling somewhere, falls down, hangs in the air, and starts spinning, spinning. . . . Again, someone knocked on the door, this time louder. . . . Then the spider overcomes the strange force, stops, swings about, hangs motionlessly, aims its beak, and falls—plummets—down to grab me with its hairy legs. . . . The knocking got even louder. . . . The fan also resembles a huge bumble-bee. It flies peacefully under the ceiling, then it hits something; everything gets mixed up and it starts buzzing, whirling from pain. . . . Someone was knocking on the door persistently. . . . I got lost in the sands of Sahara. From the top, down the slope, the wind blows; it is like a labored breathing of a boiling pot. Perhaps I was a member of an expedition, or a pilgrim; I died from thirst and they lay me down among the dunes and covered me with a dry sheet. No need to dig a hole; a white hot dune will come and bury me. . . . Loud, insistent knocking. . . . My sheet quickly dried up and the fan turned into an idiot who climbed to the upper bench in the sauna and fanned himself with a towel to cool down. If a museum of nonsense existed, I would drag the fan there. . . .

"Let's go," said the curator in a tired voice. "I will show you my museum." They entered an empty room and Edward tripped over a fan. "Keep going," encouraged the curator. Edward took a step forward, but felt emptiness under his foot. He jumped back, sat on the floor and heard a stone falling into the abyss. The curator nodded, "That's how it should be; you were afraid to encounter something and you chose to step into emptiness; you did not have time to realize that emptiness can be an abyss; you must agree that to walk around a room and suddenly fall into a mountain gorge, plunge and crash to death—is the purest kind of nonsense." "It would seem," said Edward, "that not everyone comes back from this museum." The curator nodded, "Of course, not everyone. Well, are you going to go farther?" Edward crawled away from the invisible abyss. "The walls are moving," he said, "That wall came closer exactly as much as I moved away from it." "And what does it mean?" asked the curator. "It means that your museum is ready to accommodate everything and that everything that finds its way between these walls immediately turns into nonsense. . . ."

8

He woke up. The setting sun already edged the corner of the building and, powerless to peek into the room, only gilded the dust on the glass. Apparently, that gentleman was knocking. He must have some business related to our corporation. Everything is very simple. What was I afraid of? Edward found his glasses under the pillow, threw the sheet over his shoulders and went to open the door. The elderly gentleman was standing there. He was wearing a suit and a tie, and his hand was burdened by an attache case.

"Mister Ganapati," he introduced himself.

Edward said his name without the mister and pointed to a chair next to the bed. The floor met the case with an unexpectedly loud greeting. Edward sat on the bed and their knees almost touched.

"We are dressed very differently," Edward forced out a beginning of a conversation.

"Yes, indeed," Ganapati agreed without noticing Edward's humor.

"How can you stand this heat?"

"Yes, it is quite hot," said the guest without the smallest droplet of sweat on his face.

"Excuse me, I'd better lie down."

"Go ahead," said Ganapati. He waited until Edward made himself comfortable, moved his chair closer to the bed, and locked his dark fingers. "You know, I am a mixture of a liberal and a conservative. But I am an enemy of such a latitude that it prevents a man from knowing whether his actions are good or bad. . . ."

Edward decided to shorten the introduction.

"Excuse me, I don't quite follow you. I haven't slept for two nights. Do you have some business with me? Could you, perhaps, in a few words. . . ."

"I am afraid that in a few words you will not understand."

Edward gave up, closed his eyes. The guest paused politely, but when the host failed to fill the pause, he started speaking deliberately, like a lecturer at the beginning of a long speech.

"As you probably had a chance to notice, in our country women are treated much more strictly than in the

West. This is a punishment for those freedoms, for that depraved easy life that the women of our country, the so-called *Aryans*, led thousands of years ago. . . ."

The subject of his speech was interesting, but Edward could not concentrate and kept missing entire sentences.

". . . and he filled them with passion for clothes and jewelry, with garrulity, falseness, flippancy . . . above the waist the female body was completely naked and below the waist the women wore as little as possible, like on the sculptures of Khadjuraho . . . they drank the strongest drinks, danced until late morning, were uninhibited in their relationships with men . . . they became unclean below the belly button, then unclean altogether, then the tools of the devil, the temptresses leading men astray from the path of righteousness. . . ."

Edward amused himself by creating a scenario: We'll talk for some time politely, then the man will open his case, take out the murder weapon. . . . He swallowed a bittery lump resembling a new symptom of illness, and with difficulty and even, it seemed, with a screech, turned the apples of his eyes towards the window. The dust on the glass, golden until moments before, darkened to the color of copper, as if the sun, leaning towards the horizon, kept reevaluating all the past and, like a sage at the end of his life, devalued most of it.

". . . Manu, the famed lawgiver, prescribed for them marriage when they were young, eight or ten years old, so their desires and faults did not have time to blossom, and he sent a curse on the parents in whose homes unmarried girls reached sexual maturity . . . a woman was supposed to worship her husband regardless of how bad he was, even if he was a drunk or a sadist . . . then came the custom of *suttee*—self-immolation of the widow on her husband's funeral pyre . . . even today we have the same word for a widow and for a prostitute. . . ."

Edward fell asleep. When he awoke, the guest, walking around the room, continued, with the intonation of a conclusion:

". . . the relatives of the woman and all her acquaintances would be shocked, offended, if they knew that some stranger watched her naked and, more than that, took pictures of her. . . ."

Edward sat up on the bed. "Do you want me to apologize?"

"Give me the film, and that will be the end of it. I am willing to pay you. Name your price."

"What are you saying? What does money have to do with it? You can see the veranda from here, like the palm of your own hand. I can not understand; if curious eyes from the hotel bother you, why do you allow your daughters? . . ."

"The thing is that yesterday your room sort of did not exist."

"You must be joking. . . . I've heard from several people that a year ago in the same room. . . ."

"Yesterday, a year ago—what's the difference?" For the first time, Edward could notice impatience and irritation in the guest's voice. His face tensed unpleasantly. "Precisely yesterday, or a year ago, which makes no difference to eternity, your room was not utilized yet."

It was futile to contradict such a notion.

"This veranda," said Ganapati, softening the tone of his voice and the expression on his face, "becomes popular only during summer monsoons; we watch the showers from there. But we bathe in the inner yard, which can be seen only from a helicopter, if one ever appeared above our house. Only occasionally, for various reasons, we move the barrel to the veranda, which, by the way, has good drainage; the water doesn't flood the yard, but the street. Yesterday, for example, the bricks and sand were delivered to the inner yard and we had to take the barrel up to the veranda. It is not very difficult to carry it up; we lift it up on ropes. It is more troublesome to fill it up, but our servant manages that. Before your room appeared here—I don't know what idiot got an idea to stick it on the rusty roof of the old hotel—we were comfortable on the veranda, we were well protected from the eyes of strangers. . . ."

Edward fell on the pillow and closed his heavy eyelids. A large fly was buzzing nearby. Squash it in your fingers and the guts will come out. I wish I could jump through the window. Into the barrel with water. One should live in a barrel or under showers. To be cool. . . .

"I cannot give you the film because there are other pictures on it related to my business. . . . Seriously, I don't feel good. Let's meet tomorrow morning and discuss everything. I am inviting you to breakfast. . . ."

The door slammed. Edward opened the camera, took the film out, hid it under the bed table, and immediately fell asleep. When he woke up, it was completely dark. The fan was pushing down hot air waves. Edward soaked the sheet again and lay down, but could not fall asleep. One more night in this awful room and his frail organism, weakened by insomnia and by a cold, will give the town a reason to start talking about another incident in room number eleven of the *Republic*. The plane was not leaving until the next day at noon, but Edward got up, packed his things, went down to the hall, and stepped outside. A taxi came up right away. "To the airport," ordered Edward. "It's closed already," said the taxi driver. "Then to the station." "It's closed too. . . ."

The door creaked. Somebody entered the room. "Keep down," ordered The One Who Entered, "and look around you." "There are people around me," said Edward. "Who are these people?" the visitor asked. Edward looked closely and uttered, "The girls, the magician, the hotel manager, the girls' father, the barrel-woman, and the servant. Please explain; what does it mean?" "You'll understand right away," said The One Who Entered. He gave a sign to the others, they raised something heavy, held it over Edward, and dropped it. . . .

9

A branch of a tree will sway under a bird. The buds, closed for the night, will wake up and slowly begin to open. The sleepy servant will come on the roof. He will pick up the rusty axe that only a day earlier was not rusty. The board will split noisily. Water will be poured into the barrel. A girl will run on the veranda. She'll look at the hotel's window. Behind the glass reflecting the sky will be tense emptiness. Something went wrong; something did not *come together* and— running in a straight line, in a circle, in a spiral, up or down, or in any other way—time made a mistake. Everything in this world is imperfect (only God is perfect), so why shouldn't we assume that time also has occasional breakdowns? And if we do make such an assumption, then in room number eleven of the *Republic* an axe hit the skull of a man who knew how to perceive the moments when everything in life wonderfully *came together*, but who sometimes forgot to take into account that in the balanced world the higher the mountain, the deeper the gorge; the brighter the joy, the darker the sadness; and that for each lovely harmony there exists an ugly disharmony.

But you, little girl, don't think about it. As long as your life is an unopened flower-bud, in which the straining petals don't yet know what will befall them, you better be happy that you can calmly take off your gown and, splashing, lathering, and making little showers on the veranda, play the game of lethal beauty.

Vodka and Broads

I. PRETENDER TO THE THRONE

1

The presence of an ecstatic man filled the space nearby. Addressing no one in particular, he was praising the *pirozhki*. The prince ignored him at first, for in his long and eventful life he had seen so many people that he had become too lazy to look at new ones and did not care to recognize those he had met before.

"Oh my, oh my," the man kept repeating, smacking his lips and clicking his tongue. "Look at that, what a marvel! Exactly like my mother used to bake!"

The prince extracted and put on his glasses, and did what he had not done for a long time—he looked carefully not at his own reflection in a mirror, but at another man.

"Alexander!" he cried out.

The churchgoers turned around and smiled. This meant, "The Prince, well, you know, he's getting old and mumbles to himself more and more."

Not paying attention to them, the prince greedily scrutinized his neighbor's slightly puffy face, which combined peasant and aristocratic features: deceptively sleepy blue watery eyes and a heavy nose above a thick mustache; the mighty lines of his neck and the immense chest area expressed confidence.

Finally, the old prince came to his senses. Honestly, he had not become so witless that he would forget about his friend Prince Yusupov's death half a century before. The prince coughed in embarrassment and extended his hand to the familiar stranger.

"Whom do I have the honor to meet?"

"Georgy Vampukha," the man answered with a strong handshake.

The prince saw in Vampukha several possible family relationships. First of all, Yusupov had two daughters. During the World War II, all traces of them were irretrievably lost, but if the daughters survived, got married and had children, such an encounter was not impossible; fate made him run into Yusupov's grandson. Lord! Hard to believe the resemblance! With this kind of resemblance, he should be the son.

"Allow me to ask, wouldn't you be by chance related to my friend Prince Yusupov?" the prince wanted to ask, but felt embarrassed. At the same time, it seemed to him that he *did* ask, after all. Such a confusing situation brought a grimace to the prince's face, and tiny bubbles appeared on his trembling lips.

"What did you say?" asked the stranger. "Prince Yusupov? Did you say Yusupov?"

The prince smelled alcohol.

"You must have had a drink already," he said coldly. "Before the Sunday mass?"

"Well, you see, yesterday. . . ."

"What was the occasion, if I may ask?"

"If you must know, yesterday we drank to the full moon, to Russian women, to those at sea, in prison, and in psychiatric hospitals. But excuse me, what is your name?" Vampukha smiled at the old man.

"Arseny Andreevich," the prince bowed, forgetting that he was sitting down, and as a result dipped his nose in his own plate. "And the last name—Trubetskoy."

"A famous name," said Vampukha. "The name of princes."

"I am a prince, if you want to know," Arseny Andreevich giggled and burst into a quiet laughter that dangerously strained the arteries in his brain.

In the evening of the same Sunday, the prince was writing a long letter. He got tired from this work, and his fingers hurt because he had not written as much in a long time. When he finished, he put the letter into an envelope, licked it neatly, and sealed it up. He looked for a stamp, but did not find one. He thought about the address, but could not remember it. Then, hoping to remember the address on the way, he quickly dressed to go to the post office.

Approaching the door, the prince realized that it was late, and the post office closed at five. He checked the wall clock. It was ten to midnight. The darkness outside the window confirmed that he was hopelessly late. Only when he was getting into his bed did he remember the post office was never opened on Sunday.

After breakfast (a bowl of oatmeal and two cups of coffee) Arseny Andreevich found an unopened envelope. The envelope did not have an address or a stamp. Right away he found his glasses, opened the envelope, and without sitting down started to read carefully:

"My dear old friend! How many times did I plan to write to you a detailed letter, but never did—forgive me, for God's sake! Today I am very excited; fate brought me together with your son. . . ."

He grinned, realizing he was reading his own letter.

2

Let's paraphrase Turgenev's *Smoke*: A tree is standing, and there is no wind; can the leaf on the lower branch
touch the leaf on the upper one? *No way*, you say? You're
wrong. A storm will come, everything on the tree will
get mixed up, and those two leaves will touch each other.
The storms over Russia, various storms—from political
to spiritual—scattered us in all directions, and now we
miraculously touch those who seem to be distant and
disparate, but once we touch, we realize that we are all
like the leaves of that tree.

I am forty, and I am neither a cabinet minister nor a
national celebrity, nor even an underground millionaire!
complained Vampukha to himself before he emigrated
(alluding unintentionally to the famous phrase from *Don
Carlos*, "*And nought achieved for immortality*"). True achiev-
ers, like Julius Caesar, blame only themselves for their
failures. They remake themselves and continue to move
towards their goals. Vampukha saw no flaws in himself
and blamed circumstances for his lack of success. He had
a simple explanation. He kept advancing towards his
lofty goals as he should, but the regime kept giving him
D's and F's. Therefore, he needed to find a regime able
to recognize his worth. Am I any worse than the emi-
grating Jews? Vampukha thought. If I searched deep
enough, I would also find in the Holy Land a relative
longing for me.

And so, our hero found himself in America. The regime here was considered favorable for the realization
of potential, a quality so abundantly bestowed upon all
Russians that Georgy cared little about looking for a job

and even less about finding one. He did not try to go into any business, and he did not waste time learning English. For ten years, he lived on welfare and waited for a rich person who would appreciate his soul enough to notice his diverse talents, take him under his wings, and lead him by his hand to those on whom his future would depend and who would miraculously change his life.

So far, he had not chanced upon such a man, but he did chance upon other people who could have been used. But there was a problem; relationships with them were obstructed by his limited knowledge of English. It was a vicious circle; his certainty that his generous rich man existed made learning English a waste of time; yet, without a better command of the language he was unable to develop a close relationship with rich people.

Falling into a penniless depression, Vampukha even blamed for his poor foreign language skills his high-school English teacher, with whom he parted about thirty years before. She knew the language so poorly that during class she was not ashamed to look up words in the pitiful glossary at the end of the textbook. She baffled everybody with her atrocious pronunciation; she reduced the grammar to the present and only reluctantly—to the past tense. When a curious student asked her something about the future tense, she stopped the question with her iron-tooth evil smile and asked in return, "Why do you need to know what *will be*? Anything can happen in the future! Perhaps today someone *will bury* you alive? Or *will break* your skull? Or *will drown* you in a lake?" After such an answer, the student began to relate to the future with caution and hostility. Moreover, the private life of the English teacher not only indicated, but

screamed that knowledge of English is not worth anything; like all the other women in the village, she had
problems with her hooligan son, grew potatoes, milked
the goats, got drunk on holidays and fought with her
alcoholic husband. Everybody received grades and finished the school with a feeling that to learn English well
was too complicated to even try.

Later, continuing his education at the Institute of
Physical Education, the charming burly student approached foreign languages with greater wisdom; he did
not work as much on the subject itself as on those who
taught it (thanks to a happy coincidence, all the English
professors at the Institute were young women).

In America, he would sometimes excuse his school
teacher and he would set out to acquire one of the existing quick-and-easy learning methods. On the shelves of
the bookstore were so many textbooks, tapes, and dic-
tionaries that after a short while he would come out
empty-handed and discouraged. Instead, he would immediately find his way around in an equally expansive
assortment in a liquor store. For the ten bucks allocated
to the purchase of the language aid, he was able to buy
such receptacles that after getting acquainted with their
content, he would sober up from trying to learn English
and converse brilliantly in his native language until the
last rooster crowed.

3

One Sunday morning, Vampukha was so determined
to improve his English that he went to the Russian
church, found a friendly-looking parishioner from the
first emigration, suffered through the boring conversa-

tion with him, and then asked for advice about an *effective and non-tiring aid* for learning English. The old man thought for a while; then his face beamed and he promised to bring a *simply vonderful book of dialoks* for Vampukha.

One week later, Vampukha arrived long before the beginning of the service and waited on the church porch for an hour, but the old man with the aid did not show up. Somehow, Vampukha stood through the entire service; later, in the church garden, he sat at the table with other churchgoers, ate *pirozhki*, and listened to the parishioners' complaints about America. Vampukha had many things to say on that subject and he shared with the interlocutors all of his personal resentments. The parishioners nodded their heads with sympathy, and one gentleman even moved his lips:

"Well. . . . Perhaps you shouldn't have left Russia."

Vampukha had heard such stuff before. Whenever those recent arrivals expressed dissatisfaction or disappointment, the emigrants with years of experience maliciously joined in: "Excuse me, brother, do you mean that things are not working out? You don't have enough money? Feel nostalgic? Can't find anyone to open your soul to? Missing the Russian girls? Think that all the Americans are fools? That there is no culture here? Then, what were you thinking? Let's face it, you shouldn't have emigrated; you've made a mistake." From such a blow below the belt, the recent arrivals bent in half, while the old-timers towered above them, smiling with the grins of successful engineers, accountants, Hollywood insiders, lawyers, doctors, and computer programmers.

"And if I say, for instance, that you shouldn't have been born at all?" Vampukha retorted.

"But *you* should?" exploded the gentleman and turned away from Vampukha.

"And could you answer the following?" Vampukha asked another neighbor. "After the Revolution many aristocrats left Russia, and almost all of them ended up in Europe. Why didn't they end up in America? Apparently, America rebuffed them somehow?"

"Well, as far as aristocracy is concerned, that's understandable. They used to go to Europe on vacations, to visit their relatives and friends, to improve their health, and to buy clothes; moreover, they knew French. But some of them ended up here, too." The neighbor looked around. "For instance, do you know who that old man is?" he pointed with his finger. "A real prince!"

Vampukha never saw living princes, and, obviously, never had a chance to speak to them. He asked for more *pirozhki* and carried them to the prince's table.

(From this point, the events develop exactly as they do in Chapter 1; so not to repeat ourselves, we'll move to Chapter 4).

4

Next Sunday morning, the old man who promised to bring the phrase book was sitting on a porch bench, holding a tattered booklet on his lap. Vampukha opened the book to the first page and with surprise noticed the year of publication—1914.

"Dis is trulee a vonderful book of dialoks," mumbled the representative of the first emigration. *"You shoot ignore all de new mefots. Lern by hart. I know seex leng-veedzhes, I learnt dem all by memoreezation. To learn a lengveedzh you*

don't neet to be mefodeecal. I tell you honestly, it's eeven harm-ful. My advice: open de book at random . . . and all de best!"

Finally, one day Vampukha opened the old-timer's study aid, following his advice—at random. The book consisted of parallel texts. Vampukha was immediately impressed by the approach; the student could completely ignore the phonetics, morphemics, grammar, morphology, syntax and spelling, not to mention punctuation. On the left page was the English text, and on the right— its translation into Russian. Not too eager to wrestle with English, Vampukha began to read the Russian text:

Dialog 26
In the society. Among young ladies.

(Look at that! thought Vampukha. It would be interesting to find out what young ladies talked about at the beginning of the century.)

The Butler: "Someone to see you, Miss."

"Show them in. . . . Isabella! How nice of you to come! Well, take off your coat quickly."

"I dropped in just for a moment. Mother is waiting for me in the car. Oh, you have a new coiffure! It suits you very well."

"You think so? What did you do on Friday night?"

"I went to bed early. I had a slight cold and the doctor forbade me to go out in an evening dress. Were you at Guizot's party?"

"Yes. Pity that you weren't there! We had a wonderful time. Did you know that Madame Guizot announced the engagement of her oldest daughter?"

"Really? That's news! How did you like the groom?"

"Baron von Berg? He's very nice and loves Ivette very much. It's love at first sight. Because of him, Ivette refused to marry Count Saval."

"What was Ivette wearing?"

"She had a pink dress made of thin lace. She looked quite stunning in it."

"Baron von Berg. . . . Of course, I know who he is. They say he is from Russia."

"Yes, he is Russian."

"I'm sorry for Ivette. International marriages are unhappy."

"I heard that Baron von Berg comes from a wonderful family. He is respected in St. Petersburg. Besides that, he is very rich. I can imagine how exquisite the wedding ring must be."

"What are you saying! Somebody told me that the baron is an unscrupulous adventurer looking for a wealthy fiance."

"That is all fabrication and gossip. Someone is simply very envious."

"Do you know when the wedding is to take place?"

"On Easter. The invitations will be sent soon. They say that six men from the Russian embassy will be the groom's men. And six young girls from the boarding school will be the bride's maids. . . ."

The Butler: "Excuse me, miss. Your mother asked. . . ."

"Ah, I forgot about her! I must run. Good bye. Kisses."

God, what good manners, thought Vampukha, disappointed. You can die of boredom. Why couldn't they discuss the lace on their panties? Or brag about the shape of their breasts? He wanted to finish the lesson, but the Russian baron made him anxious about something.

He read the text for a second time. Obviously, the baron had no money. The wedding ring will be exquisite, but the stone will turn out to be fake. Yet, look at the guy! He was killing two birds with one stone: he was getting the virgin Ivette, who just flew out from a boarding school, plus the wealth of her family.

Pity that he isn't a baron. . . .

Of course, Ivette was beautiful too. . . . Well, who cares about beautiful ones. Even though Vampukha respected female beauty, the money of any Ivette, even an ugly one, would push him off the reef of poverty into the ocean of real life. Then he would be able to take advantage of all the blessings of the free world. Without money, what kind of freedom are we talking about? In Russia he was much freer.

"Wouldn't you be by chance related to my friend Prince Yusupov?"

Vampukha closed his phrase book with a bang, walked around lost in thoughts, and stopped in front of a mirror. In the warm climate of California he should have walked around naked, but afraid of the unexpected, he always made sure he had underpants on. His body, athletic in the past, had become flabby and bloated, his stomach was spilling over, his face. . . . He did not even look at his face, the face of an alcoholic. But all this was nothing, it could be corrected. He should run, swim, stop stuffing himself, and cut down on alcohol. . . .

Perhaps I could become a baron too?

He finished the rest of the vodka left a day before (all in all, about three-fourths of a glass, even though the bottle looked deceptively fuller). He should think the baron idea over. A starting point already exists—Prince Arseny Andreevich. Now he must develop a plan. And then, implement it. The only problem is what, exactly, to implement. But that will come. Specificity is absurd. It keeps tossing and turning around in its unpredictable and senseless diversity. One should only choose something particular out of this infinite variety and make a wish. The most important thing in life is an idea, a dream. If you take good care of your dream, it will turn into something specific.

5

In the mornings he would drink a cup of coffee, saddle his old bicycle and drive in the direction of the mountains, to the house of Arseny Andreevich. After their first meeting, they quickly became close, surprising many parishioners. "What can there be in common," they pondered, "between an old insane prince and that one, with an unknown source of income? Perhaps the KGB is involved?"

After he learned that Vampukha relied on welfare, the prince offered his *palace*. Vampukha thought about it and decided that even though he would save on an apartment, he would partially lose his freedom; he could not have his rowdy encounters with women and friends. He thanked the prince for the offer, but explained, "I'll do it a little bit later; if I did it now, I would put my roommate in a difficult financial situation."

At first, the prince got angry, but he quickly calmed down. He would not have minded helping Vampukha financially, but, after getting to know him better, he understood that the latter would use the money to get drunk, gamble it away in Las Vegas, or spend it on women. For the sake of educating Vampukha, the prince decided to give him not even a cent, but offered him various jobs that did not pay much; he paid Georgy as much as he paid the Mexicans he had hired before that.

For some reason, neither the prince nor his friends had any easy jobs. Vampukha had to paint inside and outside, clean the yards of garbage, dig long and deep trenches, or break down the old and build the new fence, shed, awning, and whatever else could be old or new. Returning home on his bicycle, Vampukha would be dirty, tired, and angry. He would stop at a store and spend the money made that day on two bottles of the cheapest vodka and some snacks.

But all of his torments paid off one day when, while the prince was absent, he found a letter. The letter was hidden in the prince's writing desk.

My dear old friend! How many times did I plan to write you a detailed letter, but never got to it—forgive me, for God's sake! Today I am very excited; fate brought me together with your son. I came home from church, went to see the Sobkovs, had a glass of brandy and wonderful pelmeni *there, finally got home, tried to read Goncharov, but the lines kept jumping in front of my eyes and I had to put the book down. I got ready for bed and lay down, but something kept chasing sleep away from me. Finally, I got exhausted, turned on the light, took valerian drops, and now I am writing to you.*

I did not know that you had a son. And, apparently, you did not know about it either because he was born in forty-three and in forty-three you were killed. I am hastening to inform you with astonishment that your son resembles you tremendously. His first name is Georgy, last—Vampukha. It's a strange last name, for sure, but I recognized him instantly. You can clearly understand the reasons why I did not divulge my suspicions, but began to ask careful questions.

"Georgy, tell me who was your father?"

"I did not know my father, I never saw him," he answered with a shrug.

"And your mother, what did she tell you?"

"I remember my mother very little. She starved to death when I was only five. If at least a document about her death was left, I would have known when and where she was born, what was her last name, patronymic, and who my father was.

But all the papers were lost. I remember only one thing; her name was Lisa."

Well, what do you say to that? Your last lover's name was also Elizaveta! And here is what strikes me too: Elizaveta passed away in Ekaterinburg, and the tsar was also shot in Ekaterinburg. Coincidence? Who knows. But what am I saying? Of course it is coincidence.

What brought her back to Russia? I see the following scenario: At the end of the war, Elizaveta with your two-year-old son, Georgy, found herself somehow on the territory occupied by the communists, perhaps in Germany. As a Russian, as a "traitor," supposedly collaborating with the Nazis, she was arrested and sent without a trial to a labor camp in Siberia.

So that's how the things are, my friend. Your son belongs to the most recent wave of emigrants. Of course, he is in need. I will help him! I even had an idea to adopt him. You know that I do not have anyone else left. He would be my last and only heir. I willed my house and my savings to the church, but after the adoption is finalized I will immediately rewrite my will.

I still remember, as if it were yesterday, a train station in Paris and the tears of your beautiful daughters. Ah, if I could turn the clock back, to the moment when your foot so recklessly and so fatally mounted the first step of the car departing in the direction of Russia! I believe that you shouldn't have risked your life just like that. It seemed that we did everything to avoid the sad fate of those reckless aristocrats who decided to stay there. We figured out early, sagaciously, what a senseless dead-end path our dear Russia would take, how it would become destitute, and how it would self-destruct. We fled to Paris and were saved. Since we were real patriots, we did a lot to free our country.

I cannot justify your unwise action also for the following reason: if the circumstances had turned right, you could have become a serious pretender to the vacant tsarist throne. Your blood line was among the noblest, going back to Ivan the Great. You were smart, witty, honorable, with a handsome face and the body of Hercules. As far as heraldry was concerned, a few pretenders were in front of you. However, some of them died and others gave up. Yet, suddenly a much worse obstacle appeared on your path to the tsar's throne—the communist regime.

For many years we were convinced that sooner or later that regime would fall. Years went by, and nothing changed. When the war came, we started hoping that Hitler would do it. And then, you joined the ranks of the Volunteer Army and set out to free Russia. . . .

On this point the letter ended abruptly. Vampukha grabbed it, as if it were a treasure. Here it is, the winning lottery ticket, about which he was dreaming for ten years!

Blood line going back to Ivan the Great. Son of Yusupov. Tsar's throne! In today's confused Russia, miracles of many kinds are possible. . . .

Blinding the passers-by with the spokes of his bike, Vampukha dashed to the shopping center, copied the letter, returned to the prince's house, put the original in the writing desk and drove to his apartment. He was seized by joyous thoughts about the ways in which he might become an autocrat. Oh, yes, he was very aware of the semi-absurdity of his venture and of the fact that the road to the tsar's throne was highly unpredictable. However, one who doesn't try, doesn't succeed. A few happy coincidences and he'll be on his way.

At home, Vampukha was overexcited and filled his apartment with such restlessness that he felt he must get out; he had a splendid reason to party. He saddled his bicycle. . . .

A month later, he was about to jump on his bicycle to get the same stuff from the store, when he heard the telephone through the open window. In the receiver he recognized the voice of Tiurikov, his dear, but rarely seen friend. Apparently, Tiurikov longed for the company of other Russians. That was enough to have a party. In addition, Vampukha would save on alcohol; Tiurikov never came without vodka. Vampukha returned to his bicycle and rode off to buy something to eat.

II. THE GOVERNOR
OF THE ISLAND OF PAPUA

1

At last, Tiurikov reached the center of Hollywood. Here was that street, going up, weaving, with old two-story buildings divided by broken cars, laundry hanging on strings, a fat unshaven Mexican drinking beer on the porch, and black kids riding their bikes. He barely managed to park his Mercedes between two clunkers on wheels, grabbed the package with vodka and food, and walked away from the car, looking back almost as if he were saying farewell to it.

You live in a suspicious environment, my dear chap, Tiurikov thought, walking to Georgy's apartment. My friendly visits involve considerable risk. My car can be stolen or scratched; I am carrying a wallet with a couple of hundreds in cash and a dozen credit cards; and, last but not least, I am wearing pants with no holes in them and a shirt with no missing sleeves.

Vampukha opened the door not because of the doorbell; both the bell and the host preferred not to work. He opened to take the garbage out and saw Tiurikov at the door. As was his habit, Vampukha did not dress up for his guests; he had on only stretched-out underpants, and streams of sweat were running down his body. He hugged Tiurikov like a bear, and continued to dispose of the garbage.

Grimacing at the sweaty embrace, Tiurikov went inside the apartment and sat on a sagging sofa that also served as a bed. His knees pushed against a coffee table. From the mess covering the table, he extracted with his eyes a typewriter that looked as if it had been made between the wars; the connoisseurs love them, even though they are sold at garage sales for five dollars or much less or simply thrown out with the garbage. A sheet of paper was sticking out from the typewriter, and Tiurikov read there:

Georgy Vampukha
ROLLING DOWN SOMEWHERE
(a novel)

> *I am rolling down somewhere*
> *And cannot stop.*
> *Author*

Chapter One
I think I could have accomplished a lot, if, instead of wasting time on women, I had pursued more practical things. . . .

Nothing else was on the page. Next to the typewriter with the unfinished novel stood two empty bottles, one labeled *Thunderbird* and the other *Midnight Express*. Those two brands of wine were popular among the homeless and poor alcoholics because of their potency and low prices.

Tiurikov vividly imagined how Vampukha, after drinking too much, somehow collected ninety-nine cents plus seven cents tax, put his slippers on, and ran to the store at the corner. The moment he left the store, he transferred the *Thunderbird* into himself; the *bird* warmed up, flapped its wings, and flew into his soul. And what a *bird* in a soul means, especially if it is a *Russian soul*, does not require an explanation. *Midnight Express* worked equally well; in accord with its name, it sped through space under the moon. And is there a drunken Russian who does not love a fast ride?

2

Tiurikov spied two cloudy glasses with dried-up traces of old drinks, carried them to the bathroom, washed them well, and returned to the bumps of the sofa. At that moment Vampukha dashed inside. When he saw the transformed table (it was festively set with a bottle of *Absolut*, clean glasses, and a few cans of hors d'oeuvres that Tiurikov bought in the grocery store), his face, washed out by alcohol and an unbalanced diet, became more focused.

Then, the glass turned into an icon, a point of convergence for Vampukha's eyes, fingers, lips, and soul. Not brought up as a Christian, Georgy Vampukha, like many other Russians, satisfied his soul's desire to become enlightened and exalted not through prayer, but through alcohol. He did not gulp all the vodka in the glass, but took two slow sips and placed the glass on the table.

This ceremonial approach did not indicate a custom or mannerism. He had not yet forgotten the course of treatment for chronic alcoholism, which, at the state's expense, having the status of a person in financial need, he underwent about half a year before.

"What are you doing?" Tiurikov teased him. "You're drinking like an American."

Being accused of forgetting some important Russian custom was so unbearable for Vampukha that he literally gulped what was left in the glass, spilling some on his chest and the table. And without taking an hors d'oeuvre, he rushed to attend the boiling pot on the stove.

Usually he cooked simpler dishes, but for such a rare guest he prepared a Bavarian roast. Vampukha was an intuitive cook; he combined everything—the ingredients and their quantity—by eye, but his food always came out tasty. The concrete knowledge (for instance, how long or at what temperature to cook) was positively harmful to him. When he read that a roast should be cooked five hours, he complied, and later could only complain: It was tiring, the cooking took too long, the guests were hungry and had to drink on empty stomachs. And very often they got drunk before the roast was ready or after it was burned to a crisp.

Once, at midnight, walking home through deserted and scared Hollywood, he got to talk to a woman at a bus stop. She was from Germany and knew English better than Vampukha, but she was not able to explain what brought her to the City of Angels. She was trying to finish a bottle of *Midnight Express* and kept complaining about the lack of cocaine. He helped her with the wine, but could not help with the coke. She agreed that a bed is much better than a dirty bench, and she lived with Vampukha for two weeks, teaching him how to make the Bavarian roast and *accidentally* stabbing him with a knife in the cramped kitchen *while cutting the beef* (that's how he explained the scar on his chest). After that she vanished suddenly. Her recipe allowed Vampukha to cook the Bavarian roast much faster—not in five hours, but only in two.

3

"Tastes like a dream," Tiurikov praised the roast, swallowing the first piece. "And how is Marat? Still painting the church?"

"Should I call him?" asked Vampukha. "I'll tell him that you're here and he'll come right away. We just talked about you yesterday. Where, says he, is Tiurikov? He's doing things, I say. He has, I say, important things on his mind, while we have nothing but vodka and broads."

Vodka and Broads, Tiurikov thought. Here's a wonderful title to Vampukha's unfinished novel. *Rolling Down Somewhere* reveals the idea, but is too straightforward. Straightforwardness is always artificial since there are no straight lines in life and in our lives we all move in zigzags. And *Vodka and Broads* hits the point. I am not a monk either, but how can I, an exhausted businessman, find time for these pleasures? In Russia, I played piano in a traveling orchestra, and when I was in the mood, I gave lessons; in Russia, I had more time than I knew what to do with. I wanted to be a musician in America, but then I looked more carefully and realized that an average musician here either has to resign himself to being poor, learn to be a computer programmer, or perhaps become a businessman. I could not get used to poverty and I chose the latter option. Vampukha also doesn't accept poverty, but he can live with it. And here an interesting casus appears; even though materially we've both arranged our affairs differently, we are both dissatisfied with life. He envies my money and I envy his life without responsibilities, schedules, appointments, investments, and rat races. Which of us is right; which of us lives more wisely?

"In one thing you are absolutely wrong," he continued his reflections aloud. "In your attitude to the English language. The dust of your motherland should be brushed off no later than on the Aeroflot plane, and here you should immerse yourself from the first day in the local population. And even if you want to get drunk here, I would recommend getting drunk with Americans. At least your English would improve."

"How can you say that I'm not getting immersed? You've seen how many female representatives of the local indigenous population I fucked!"

"I know them, your local females. They are alcoholics, bums, and wackos. Tell me, did you ever try to calculate your chances of achieving success? I am not talking here about picking up women, but about greater goals. Think about it; statistically speaking, half of the human race belongs to the female sex. And half of this half, that is, a quarter of the entire human population, is stopping you from advancing, without even lifting a finger, just by its physical presence. Conclusion: it does not matter where you go, under what regime you find yourself—every fourth human being interferes with your reaching your goal. You were lucky or unlucky that you were born a Casanova. What is important is *how* we use those assets that we brought into this world—with a sense of purpose or without it. . . . You should learn from Vladas," Tiurikov pointed to the sofa in the opposite corner of the room.

The sofa belonged to the Lithuanian, but Tiurikov never had a chance to see him. Vladas worked simple jobs with complex schedules just to save ten thousand dollars for his move to his beloved Sweden. His variant of parting with the Soviet Union was one of the riskiest; in the winter he crossed the border somewhere in the region of the Finnish marshes. Avoiding the Finns, he reached Sweden and asked for political asylum. Sweden seemed to have taken him in, but a certain emigre from Russia had got him confused. "What is Sweden," he used to say, "with its all-pervading socialism? We did not run away *from there* to step into socialist shit again. But America—yes; there, an enterprising person is able to find real capitalism and unrestricted possibilities." Who could voluntarily deny being enterprising? Persuaded, the Lithuanian left for America and enterprised for some time feverishly wherever he could; yet, everywhere he invariably went bust, and finally began to remember with tenderness the delights of Swedish socialism.

"Vladas does not go after millions, but stubbornly, persistently, and patiently pursues his goal. Look, you are drinking, and what is Vladas doing? Vladas is making money to go to his beloved Sweden. Once there, he'll look around and he'll stay, regardless of the toughness and impossibility of getting a break in their emigration policies. And I have a suspicion about what he'll do to become a Swedish citizen. He'll go to a god-forsaken place on the shore of a beautiful fjord; there, he'll meet a girl, exactly like the one every man is dreaming about from the time he is born. Of course, she will be a blonde, as almost all Swedish girls are, and her eyes will be, of course, blue. Imagine, you are going somewhere along the fjord and a Swedish girl is walking towards you; her hair is light, the color of platinum, it smells of flowers, warm milk, hay, and snow; the smell of her hair can drive you mad, and her eyes can kill you on the spot. . . ."

Tiurikov paused to make Vampukha feel even more acutely the huge difference between the strumpets of Los Angeles, from whom he could get AIDS (if he already hadn't gotten it), and the angel living on the shore of the fjord.

"But Vladas won't be picky. He'll stop any girl to ask her a question. For instance, he'll ask how deep is the fjord or what kind of bird is flying above. Pretty girls like nature, everybody in Sweden knows English, so their conversation probably will work out and soon the girl (if not the first then perhaps the tenth) will become his wife. . . ."

Vampukha moved in his thoughts to an inflatable mattress floating on the water's surface, and he looked at Tiurikov as if he were a cloud. He was listening to the babbling of his friend's words, but did not try to understand their meaning. Tiurikov decided to shake him up:

"I'm curious about what are you thinking when you don't have money to go out? You don't only drink and write your novel, do you? Share with me your latest ideas. And perhaps teach me something; for instance, what, in your opinion, one needs to do to become rich quickly?"

One needs to become the tsar, Vampukha would have said if the conversation had taken place a week earlier. Well, even then he wouldn't have said that; he'd have bitten his tongue no matter how much he'd had to drink. Tactful Tiurikov wouldn't have laughed at every crazy idea, but the idea of becoming the tsar would prove too much even for him.

"One needs to get married," answered Vampukha. "However, not to a poor Swedish beauty, but to some rich old woman. It is fashionable now for women to have a much younger lover. Consider the discussions on TV shows: she is fifty, he is nineteen, and they love each other, like Romeo and Juliet; what do you say to that, ah? I am forty-eight, so add thirty more, and my partner should be seventy-eight. The older, the better; ninety would be perfect. Think about the situation of that old woman. She has plenty of money, but she is lonely; she wants some attention and understanding. Her servant changes her light bulbs, but can you compare a tender male hand to the hand of a maid from Guatemala? I will change the light bulb, jump off the chair, pat her on her grey-haired head and kiss her parchment-like hand. As in a nostalgic old movie. I will drop in front of her on my knees and tenderly look for a long time in her colorless short-sighted eyes. . . ."

"But tell me why," interrupted Tiurikov, "there are many aged and lonely women millionaires in the world, but there are even more young and nice poor men? Why don't they, I'd like to know, run into each other?"

"Because young poor men are stupid. They are afraid that people will gossip, 'We know, we know why he needs the old woman.' Or they are fussy. Idiots! They should be fussy about poverty and their stupefying, low-paying jobs. Instead, here you have a nice granny who will give you tasty morsels, dress you, take you to Florida, Hawaii, or Carnegie Hall. In general, why shouldn't one look at it this way: I did not marry an old hag, but found myself a granny?"

"So why don't you have a granny yet?"

Vampukha smiled mysteriously.

"Well?" Tiurikov urged him on.

4

Not long before, walking through Beverly Hills in the midst of the fabulous mansions, Vampukha waved his hand at a Rolls Royce because he noticed some female silhouettes behind its tinted windows.

For a long time, from the days of his youth, he routinely followed a maxim that the more often you smile at women, the more women you get. In Russia, where he was younger, worked as an assistant to a movie director and had friends and useful connections, his predilection for the weaker sex was delightfully inexhaustible and he was satisfied with the equation *one hit in ten*. In America, all this changed for the worse; here he had to make peace with the equation *one woman out of a hundred*.

And suddenly, he got lucky; the Rolls Royce turned around and came close, the window in the back rolled down and revealed the smiling female faces of undetermined nationality. The faces were definitely far from being young, but they were exotic and well groomed.

"Haw doo yoo doo?" said Vampukha, using his best English.

"Hi," said the woman closest to him in a low and hoarse voice of a chain smoker. "You have a strange accent."

"I am from Russia," said Vampukha. "And you?"

"From Tahiti," said one of the women.

"Tahiti is a wonderful country!"

"What's your name?" they asked him.

"Dzhordzh. And yours?"

He recognized the name of the one who was closest to him.

"Margarita is my favorite name."

He wrote his telephone number, handed the note to Margarita, pressed her wrinkled hand to his lips. He rated the possibility of a call from the Tahitian at one percent and was astonished when, a month later, the hoarse female voice in the receiver invited him *for a cup of coffee.*

Margarita lived on the ocean. Since no direct bus went there, Vampukha had to transfer. After he found out that he had to wait at least one hour for the next bus, he stretched out to take a nap on the bus-stop bench, but at that moment some bum sat at his feet and started mumbling something. Disgusted, Vampukha walked away, saw a little liquor store, bought a pocket-size bottle of *Smirnov*, and shortened his wait sipping vodka and turning his eyes away from the bum, who stared at the bottle.

Margarita had an apartment in a beautiful high-rise building overlooking the marina and the ocean. Unfortunately, the hostess was not alone, but in the company of a few girlfriends. They reprimanded Vampukha for being late, gave him a cup of cappuccino, and offered cookies and fruit. Annoyed by the unexpected company and the lack of any liquor, he apathetically sipped his cappuccino, chewed on diet cookies, and listened to insipid conversations, missing a lot of them. And suddenly he understood *my islands.*

"Yes," Margarita confirmed, "I do have a few islands."

"You bought them?"

"Inherited them from my father."

"If I only could," said Vampukha, "live on an island for a while. . . ."

"Why not? Whenever you want. Do you want me to make you a governor? You'll govern the Papuans."

Vampukha imagined the half-naked Papuan women with whom he did whatever he wanted, and he agreed enthusiastically. Then, he excused himself and went to the restroom to finish the leftover *Smirnov.* He was about to drop the bottle in the waste basket, but changed his mind and put the empty bottle in his back pocket. Apparently, he did not put it there carefully enough because when he was getting into his chair, the bottle squeezed out from the pocket and fell on the floor.

Vampukha's embarrassment did not last long. *Smirnov* was doing its job. Soon he recovered completely and tried to rehabilitate himself by telling lies often tried before: he was a talented Russian poet, beloved by the people, but not by the government; he was in danger of ending up in a mental hospital or in the Gulag; but, you understand, we have only one life, and for that reason he unwillingly ran away to the West; and in a foreign country, as you can understand, in the beginning everything is quite difficult.

Finally, the girlfriends went to the foyer. He moved to the sofa and sprawled comfortably on the pillows. The farewell din finally ended and his hostess returned to the living room. But instead of being glad to see the man's transparent hint, she removed the smile from her face, did not stay neutral, but continued to change her expression to more and more furious, and with poorly concealed annoyance, she began to speak about some urgent business. Vampukha overcame his disappointment; at the door he looked in Margarita's eyes with the tenderness of a man in love, paid her compliments, and kissed her hand.

Since that moment he had called Margarita perhaps a hundred times and unfailingly got the answering machine; he spoke warmly to the machine, but the Tahitian did not call him back.

Once, after fortifying his bravery with the tried procedure, he splurged on a bouquet and appeared at Margarita's. The guard sitting in the vestibule listened patiently to the story of a nephew who suddenly arrived from Europe, called his auntie Margarita and had a conversation with the answering machine. Then he sarcastically suggested that "to save on gas ('on a taxi,' Vampukha corrected him), well then, to save on a taxi, one should first call, and only then come to see *them*."

5

"Vodka and broads," nodded Tiurikov. "Not a bad mix, but a risky one. Together with the bottle, you dropped your reputation on the floor."

Vampukha stared into the empty bottle. The emptiness that replaced the consumed vodka merged with the emptiness that remained after his crazy, but vivid dream of ascending to the vacant throne of the tsar. In the evening Vampukha would often come to spend the night at the prince's, but earlier he would come alone, and that time he brought a wench with him. The night would have turned out great, but the stupid woman did not know how to whisper and did not want to stop giggling. Even though the prince was hard of hearing, the squealing female awakened him; when he went downstairs, he found his proposed heir making love to a black woman. Angry, he asked them both to get out. Vampukha was offended by this treatment; he did not leave and he kept the girl. Furious, the prince wrote Vampukha a letter, in which he sarcastically criticized his loose nature, and, in addition, accused him of stealing approximately two hundred dollars (which Vampukha did not steal, but simply discreetly borrowed, to return later, of course).

Vampukha recovered from that failure with the help of the following rationale. It appeared that communism had crumbled and a different system, as yet difficult to understand, was forming in Russia; but the main obstacle to the return of the tsar was the unwillingness of the government to share power with anyone else. Moreover, the people became completely different. They had changed a lot since the revolution and did not need another boss, especially one with dictatorial aspirations.

Emptiness, as we know from school physics, does not like to remain empty, but it tries to fill up as quickly as possible, and it is not at all concerned with what. In Vampukha's case, the emptiness filled up with verses he learned in his youth. He lifted his hands theatrically and quoted with passion:

"The secrets of eternity are not revealed to mortals. Then what should we do? Love and drink wine?"

"We should run to the store," he expanded Omar Khayyam's lines, pulled on a pair of shorts and a T-shirt, and was ready to drive, run, walk, stumble, even crawl to get the second, and, hopefully, not the last, bottle.

That's why I come back here, risking my car and my wallet, thought Tiurikov, admiring the optimistic spirit of his friend. It is as if I were coming back to Russia.

They walked out into the darkness full of cicadas, got into the Mercedes, which had not been stolen, bought in the closest store a couple of bottles of *Stolichnaya*, and later, drinking straight from the bottle, they drove half the night around Hollywood looking for any available women (which, as we know, are plentiful, but never when you really need them).

In the morning, Vampukha woke up for a moment, could not recall any obligations, slept till noon, went to get some wine, and prepared himself a nice meal from the remaining hors d'oeuvres and the roast. When his physical condition improved and he began to feel the *bird* in his soul, he dressed up in his best clothes and went on foot to Beverly Hills, a world symbol of wealth and fame.

Walking until he got bored, he kept saying hello to old women leaving the prestigious stores and expensive cars. He knew enough English words to ask how to get here or there, say a compliment and even lie that he was a famous movie director who recently arrived from Russia. Saying good-bye, he would hand them his telephone number, tenderly look in their eyes, and kiss their wrinkled hands.

* * *

Wouldn't this be a good place to finish our story? Or perhaps, just out of politeness, we should mention what

happened to Tiurikov? But honestly, who could be interested in the life of an American Philistine into whom,
according to Vampukha, Tiurikov was turning dangerously quickly? "These boring Americans," say many recent Russian emigres, "live hiding their heads in the sand;
they do not see further than the tip of their own noses.
They are superficial, narrow-minded people. We, on the
contrary, do things in a big way; we have natural know-
how and a rich culture. And they can't even come close
to our spirituality!"

And truly, a businessman's day is very boring. Our
Tiurikov would get up in the morning, drink his coffee,
eat something, and immediately, still yawning and with
a headache, he would have to sit down in his office in
front of his computer. Then he'd begin calling his clients, read his new mail, write a few checks, drive to see
his accountant, take the copier to get fixed . . . and in this
manner he would spend his entire day doing things for
which he had no heart and no mind. Three more months
would speed by in exactly the same bustle and our
Tiurikov would be fed up with everything to such a degree he would try to save himself, using a safety-valve
with the robust name Vampukha.

And again—the sinking sofa, a battery of bottles on
the table, the beginning of *Rolling Down Somewhere*,
vodka, the tasty roast, intimate conversations about the
opposite sex, and the question, formulated approximately as follows, "Of course, it is great to have money,
but how tedious it is to make it. So share with me your
latest ideas. How can one quickly, easily, and perhaps
even pleasantly make a million dollars?"

Vampukha will smile mysteriously.

**FLAMINGO
BOOKS**